"I don't like your attitude,"

Julie said, setting the pan on the burner with more force than necessary.

"I'm not exactly thrilled with yours, either. You have a huge chip on your shoulder, and it's obvious you're itching for a fight." Matt leaned forward as if to kiss her, then pulled away. "So go on. Tell me what you think of me."

"Why are you here anyway?" Julie asked, avoiding his question.

"Cooking lessons, remember?"

"You seem a little more interested in flirting than cooking."

Matt tilted his head. "Sorry. I can't seem to help myself. I don't usually come on so strong. But there's something between us. I can feel it. I think you can, too." He leaned back against the counter, folding his arms in front of him. "Desire, intense, irrational desire."

Dear Reader,

The summer is over, it's back to school and time to look forward to the delights of autumn—the changing leaves, the harvest, the special holidays . . . and those frosty nights curled up by the fire with a Silhouette Romance novel.

Silhouette Romance books always reflect the laughter, the tears, the sheer joy of falling in love. And this month is no exception as our heroines find the heroes of their dreams—from the boy next door to the handsome, mysterious stranger.

September continues our WRITTEN IN THE STARS series. Each month in 1991, we're proud to present a book that focuses on the hero—and his astrological sign. September features the strong, enticingly reserved Virgo man in Helen R. Myers's *Through My Eyes*.

I hope you enjoy this month's selection of stories, and in the months to come, watch for Silhouette Romance novels by your all-time favorites including Diana Palmer, Brittany Young, Annette Broadrick and many others.

We love to hear from our readers, and we'd love to hear from *you!*

Happy Reading,

Valerie Susan Hayward
Senior Editor

KRISTINA LOGAN

Hometown
Hero

Silhouette **Romance**

Published by Silhouette Books New York

America's Publisher of Contemporary Romance

To my favorite ballplayer, Terry

SILHOUETTE BOOKS
300 E. 42nd St., New York, N.Y. 10017

HOMETOWN HERO

ISBN: 0-373-08817-5

First Silhouette Books printing September 1991

Books by Kristina Logan

Silhouette Romance

Promise of Marriage #738
Hometown Hero #817

KRISTINA LOGAN

is a native Californian and a former public-relations professional who spent several exciting years working with a variety of companies whose business interests ranged from wedding consulting to professional tennis, high technology and the film industry. Now the mother of two small children, she divides her time between her family and her first love, writing.

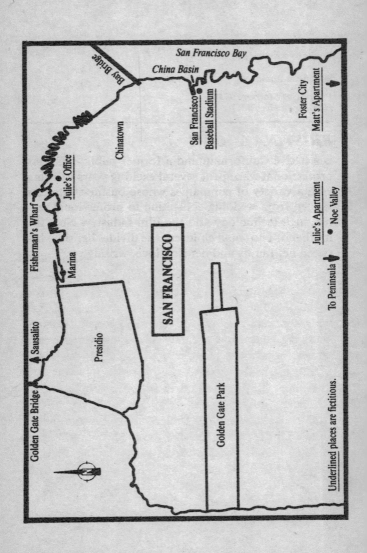

San Francisco Bay

China Basin

Bay Bridge

San Francisco
Baseball Stadium

Foster City
Matt's Apartment →

Chinatown

Julie's Office

Fisherman's Wharf

Marina

Sausalito →

Golden Gate Bridge

Presidio

SAN FRANCISCO

Julie's Apartment • Noe Valley

To Peninsula →

Golden Gate Park

Underlined places are fictitious.

Chapter One

"**I** need a man," Angela Moretti announced, opening the door to Julie's office. "Handsome, rich, talented and famous, and you're going to get him for me."

Julie Michaels smiled. "Sure I am. Right after I find one for myself." She pushed a stack of brochures across her small, cluttered desk. "Why don't you make yourself useful and stamp our return address on the back."

Angela pushed the offending pile away. "We can do those later. Right now we have a bigger problem."

"Finding you a man?"

"Not me, the foundation." She slid into the chair in front of Julie's desk, her lighthearted manner turning serious. "Our Celebrity Cook-off is turning into a local show with no pizzazz. We have every politician in the San Francisco Bay Area willing to participate, but not one person with any real clout."

"I thought you just signed Stefan Morino."

"He's a violinist, Julie. Not that I have anything against musicians, but I hardly think he's going to bring in the masses. We need someone bigger than life—a hero."

"I suppose you have someone in mind," Julie asked, her attention still focused on the stack of brochures she had to fold and stamp before the afternoon mail delivery.

"Yes. Matt Kingsley."

Julie shook her head. "No way. I am not going to do it."

"You don't even know what I'm going to ask."

"I'm afraid I do. You want me to use my baseball connections to get Matt Kingsley for the cook-off. I thought I had made myself perfectly clear on this subject." Julie stared down at her desk, hating the feeling of guilt that was already swamping her.

"I'm desperate," Angela said quietly. "You know how important this fund-raiser is for the foundation. It's the backbone of our budget, and quite frankly, expenses have been much higher than we expected this year. If we don't pull in a significant amount of funds at the cook-off, we may have to shut down some of our programs."

Julie leaned back against her chair with a sigh. "But why Matt Kingsley? There are hundreds of celebrities in San Francisco who will bring in a crowd."

"Because he's hot. He's the ace hitter for the Cougars, and he practically won the division title single-handedly last year, not to mention the fact that he recently signed a multimillion dollar baseball contract. The man has everything we want. He's talented, famous and he appeals to everyone from the business executive to the mail room clerk. He's a legend in the making. The press loves him. The fans love him. Heck, I even love him.''

Julie stood up, walked over to the window and gazed blankly out at the colorful crowds strolling along Fisherman's Wharf. She had had enough of baseball legends to last a lifetime. Her father, Jack Michaels, had been one of the greatest pitchers in the National League. She turned back to face Angela. ''He's a baseball player, not a god.''

''Tell that to my ten-year-old nephew and my sixty-five-year-old aunt. They both love him.''

''So call and ask him.''

''I have called him, about a hundred times. I can't get past his agent. Actually I can't get past his agent's secretary.''

''Neither can I,'' Robert Hudson announced, pushing his way into Julie's office.

Julie looked at the executive director in dismay. Robert Hudson was a friend, but he could also be ruthless when it came to the foundation. He was determined to make the California Chapter of the National Children's Foundation a showcase of success, and he would stop at nothing to make that happen, including infringing on a friendship.

''It's time to bring in the big guns,'' he said.

She shook her head. ''I want to help, but—''

''We need Matt Kingsley,'' Robert said with determination. ''I don't care how you get him, just get him.'' His words echoed through the room, and then he turned and walked away.

''Robert always did like to make an exit,'' Angela commented. ''What are you going to do?''

Julie's mouth twisted into a grim smile. ''Get Matt Kingsley.''

* * *

A car horn blared in her ear, and Julie instinctively hit the brakes in front of the entrance to the San Francisco baseball stadium. Muttering under her breath, she put her foot back down on the gas and pulled into the parking lot as a carload of three teenage girls hurtled past her.

Her own Honda cruised at a more leisurely pace, reflecting the hesitancy of her mission. She didn't want to be at the ballpark on this beautiful springtime day. She had no interest in watching batting practice or joining the groupies crowded around the players' entrance, but she had no choice—she had tried everything else.

For two days she had called Matt Kingsley's agent, but the man was always unavailable. She had tried every ploy imaginable, calling at off-hours or during lunchtime in the hope that the ever-efficient secretary would be away from her desk and that Sam Blakely would answer the phone himself. But nothing had worked. Her messages were duly recorded with the standard answer that Mr. Blakely would return her call if Mr. Kingsley was interested in participating in the event—in other words, no.

With a sigh she pulled into a parking space just to the right of the main gate and got out of the car, slamming the door in an attempt to release some of her anxiety. She had finally given in to the inevitable. She was going to have to use her connections. Dale Howard was the general manager of the Cougars, and one of her father's best friends. Of course he hadn't returned her calls, either, but perhaps a personal visit would spark his memory.

As she walked through the archway of the main gate, the queasiness in her stomach grew as the memories returned. The stadium was silent, but in her mind she could hear the cheers and applause of game day, she could smell the hot dogs and onions and she could feel the damp windiness of the walkways. A shiver shot through her body as she remembered the long nights at the ballpark, falling asleep in her mother's arms, her stomach filled with popcorn and pretzels. They should have been happy memories, but they were tinged with pain and betrayal.

She tried to shrug off the bad feelings, but everywhere she looked brought back a memory, and she was surprised by the number of people at the ballpark for an off-season batting practice session. Angela had been right. The Cougars were the hottest game in town, even when they weren't playing.

When she saw the crowd of adoring women waiting in front of the players' entrance, she wanted to flee. It was so familiar it was frightening. She could see herself as a young girl following proudly behind her father. He had been her hero then.

Shaking her head, she turned away and walked up to the club offices. She paused in the reception area, and gave her name to the young woman behind the desk.

"Do you have an appointment with Mr. Howard?" the woman asked.

"No, but I just need a few minutes of his time. I'm an old friend."

The woman looked at her skeptically. "Sorry, but he's not here. Batting practice ended fifteen minutes ago. Would you like to leave a message or a phone number?"

"Sure." She recited her name, number, and a brief message for Dale Howard to get in touch, which the secretary dutifully recorded. "I don't suppose I could speak to Matt Kingsley."

"Only if you're his mother, father or agent."

"That's what I thought. Thanks, anyway."

Julie walked slowly out into the sunshine. She hated to go back to the office without having accomplished anything. Robert and Angela would be very disappointed.

When she reached the lower level, she noticed that the group around the players' entrance had grown since she'd arrived. She paused on the outskirts, another idea forming in her mind as she moved into the crowd.

"Hey, wait your turn," a young girl snapped as she tried to get to the front of the line. The girl pushed her aside, driving an elbow into her rib cage, and as Julie winced in pain, two more girls pushed their way past her. She was buried in the middle of the crowd.

She had to stand on tiptoe to see over the people in front of her, and she began to realize the foolishness of her sudden brainstorm. Matt Kingsley wasn't going to just stop and chat with her, not with this mass of women waiting outside the entrance. She was just turning to leave when the door opened and two young men walked out.

The freshness of their smiles as they looked at the women was enough to tell her that neither was the infamous Matt Kingsley. They were too caught up in the excitement to be the veteran ace hitter for the ball club.

They stopped to sign a few autographs, reveling in the attention. One of the young girls went so far as to climb over the barricade in an attempt to steal a kiss. A guard immediately came to the player's aid, but no one seemed to be in a hurry to break the embrace.

Julie turned away in disgust. This approach was definitely not going to work. She had known that all along. She had seen her father dodge enough wild fans to know that Matt Kingsley wasn't going to just waltz through this pack of wolves.

She looked around for a side door. The San Francisco stadium was new, and she wasn't familiar with the setup, but she had enough experience to know that there were other ways for the players to leave.

"Excuse me," she called out to one of the guards.

"Yeah?"

"Is Matt Kingsley here today?"

The other girls fell silent, waiting breathlessly for his answer.

"No, he didn't come."

There was a general murmur of disappointment, but Julie was the only one who turned to leave. She was relieved in a way. Just being at the ballpark reminded her of the hesitant, awkward young girl she had once been. She didn't like that feeling of being unsettled. She was a confident, mature woman now, not a silly schoolgirl with some shattered dreams.

Her heels clicked against the concrete as she walked out to her car. It was then that she spotted a very tall, well-built man striding toward a bright red Ferrari parked well away from the other cars. She knew instantly that she had found her man. Everything about him from the stylishly cut brown hair to the tan and the tight blue jeans spelled superstar.

In that split second, she didn't stop to think about his reaction, she just plunged forward, anxious to get the job done before she lost her nerve. She reached him just as he got to the door of his car. Breathlessly, she grabbed the sleeve of his sweater, feeling once again like that foolish schoolgirl.

"Mr. Kingsley. Wait, please. I need to talk to you."

He looked down at her in surprise, his face much grimmer than she had expected.

"What?" he demanded.

She looked into his light green eyes and felt the breath catch in her throat. No wonder the man was a star. He was gorgeous.

"Do you want an autograph?" he asked briskly, removing her hand from his sleeve.

"No. I want you," she mumbled, saying the first thing that came into her mind as she stared into his incredibly sexy eyes.

"Sorry, I'm not available. Why don't you try one of the guys over there." He pointed to a group of players now talking to the crowd, and then started to slide into his car. She reached for his arm, her fingers locking onto the knit of his sweater in frustration. She was acting like a star-struck idiot.

"No, wait. I don't mean you, exactly. I just want to talk to you. I have to ask you something—"

"Not today, sweetheart. I don't have time. Please let go of my sleeve." His voice was filled with polite weariness.

Julie looked down at her hand where she was unconsciously twisting his sweater. She hadn't felt this tongue-tied in years. It was inconceivable that a baseball player had reduced her to this; she should have her head examined. She tried again.

"My name is Julie."

"Look, honey, I don't care what your name is. In fact, I think it's better if I don't know. Please just go away. I'm tired. I just want to go home and go to bed. Alone.''

"I just want to talk to you for a minute," she said in exasperation.

"Talk? That's a new one."

"Mr. Kingsley—"

"If I give you what you want, will you leave?"

"Yes, of course," she snapped, unaware of his intentions, until he took her into his arms. "What—what do you think you're doing?"

"Giving you what you want," he growled into her ear as his lips covered hers in a long, hot kiss.

"Stop it. Just stop it." She felt more shaken than angry. It should have been easy to pull away from him, but for just a moment she had felt herself respond to the warmth of his mouth, the sexy brush of his mustache against her lips.

He looked at her in surprise, and then his eyes traveled down her body, taking in the peach-colored linen suit, the sheer stockings and high heels. He had been too weary to really notice her before. She wasn't a teenager; she was a beautiful young woman with golden hair and fiery brown eyes.

His hands fell from her shoulders as he stared at her warily. "Okay."

"That's it? Okay? You kiss me and then say 'okay'?"

Matt smiled at her annoyance, suddenly beginning to enjoy the unusual encounter. "Sorry. Just trying to please."

"You're the most arrogant man I've ever met." It was a standard line to fall back on, but the only one she could think of at the moment. "You have a lot of nerve."

He didn't seem at all put off by her remarks. "You said you wanted me," he reminded her, his interest in her deepening with every second.

"I certainly didn't ask you to kiss me." Her indignant protest brought another smile to his lips.

"I guess we got our signals crossed. I thought you were a fan. But come to think of it, you don't look like a groupie, you don't talk like one and you certainly don't kiss like one."

Julie's mouth dropped open at his provocative statement. "What do you mean, I don't kiss like a groupie?" She mentally kicked herself for asking such a leading question. What difference did it make what he thought of the way she kissed? He was a baseball player. "Forget I asked that."

He shrugged. "Fine. So, who are you and what do you want?"

She stared at him blankly, finally realizing that she was going to be given an opportunity to explain. She took a deep breath, taking a minute to regain her poise. "My name is Julie Michaels," she stated briskly. "I work for the California Children's Foundation. I came to see you, hoping I could persuade you to participate in our fund-raiser. I know you're very busy, but—"

His smile faded into a frown. "I am busy."

"It's for a good cause."

He shook his head. "They all are. I wish I could help you, but right now I need to concentrate one hundred percent on baseball. Another time, perhaps, but not now."

"It's only one night. A couple of hours. And it would mean so much." She hated herself for begging, but it was important that he realize what was at stake. "The kids, they—"

"I said no," he snapped.

"Don't you even want to know what it's all about, where the money goes? Don't you have time to hear about the people who would benefit from your appearance?"

"I'm sure it's a good cause. But there are a lot of good charities out there. I can't do it. I'm sorry." His words came out much colder than he intended, but he had spent the past month fulfilling commitments, and he wanted to concentrate on baseball, nothing else.

"The season doesn't start for six weeks," she protested, knowing it was useless. He was a baseball player; she shouldn't have been surprised at his attitude. Her father had never gone out of his way to help the little guy.

"Hey, I said I was sorry. Baseball comes first."

His words struck a deeply buried memory.

"You're sorry?" She shook her head, the words pouring out of her before she could stop herself. "I don't think so, Mr. Kingsley. I think you're just so caught up in your own star-studded world that you can't think about anybody besides yourself. You're worrying about hitting a little ball over a fence, and we're trying to help children survive cancer operations and child abuse. God, I hate macho baseball players," she said passionately, her voice ringing through the parking lot.

Matt stared at her in surprise. No one had ever talked to him like that.

"Look, there he is," a young girl shouted from the distant crowd as their argument drew attention.

Julie whirled around as the crowd turned toward them, their adoring faces filled with excitement. He was their hero, a man who rose above all others, but she

couldn't see what they saw, or maybe she just didn't
want to.

The drive from the baseball stadium in China Basin
to the foundation offices near the wharf gave her time
to think, and the anger was slowly replaced by guilt and
embarrassment. She had never spoken like that to anyone. But Matt Kingsley's curt refusal had opened up the
old wounds, had reminded her of all the times her father had said no to her because baseball came first.

She banged the steering wheel in frustration. When
was she going to be free of the man? It had been eight
years since she had seen her father, eight years since she
had attended a baseball game or had played the game,
but the mere mention of the sport sent her emotions
spinning out of control. Within minutes she changed
from a calm, poised businesswoman into a foolish
young girl. She couldn't begin to imagine what Matt
Kingsley thought of her irrational behavior.

Her guilt deepened as she walked into the office and
saw Robert and Angela setting up the foundation slide
show in the conference room. The three of them were a
team. In two years they had turned the foundation into
a successful organization and had widened the scope of
their programs to include not only physical health but
also mental and emotional health of children up and
down the state. They had done it by pulling together, by
working long hours and most of all by being nice to the
right people.

They looked up expectantly as she pushed open the
door.

"I'm sorry," she said.

Angela nodded understandingly. "You didn't see
him."

"Damn." Robert shook his head in frustration. "We need that man." His mind started whirling with ideas. "We'll have to try something else. I found out last night that he goes to the Royal Athletic Club every morning between six and eight o'clock. That might be a good spot to get to him."

"I don't think so," Julie replied.

Robert looked at her in surprise, his eyes reflecting his displeasure. "You're not giving up. This is too important."

"I did see Matt Kingsley." She took a deep breath. "I spoke to him. He said no, and then—then I insulted him." Julie pulled out a chair and sat down, her legs suddenly feeling weak with delayed reaction.

"You didn't," Angela breathed.

"I'm afraid so."

"What exactly do you mean—you insulted him?" Robert asked sharply.

"I asked him to participate in the fund-raiser, and he said no. He didn't say maybe. He said no. And then I got angry. He wouldn't even give me a chance to explain, to tell him what we're all about." Her normally soft voice was filled with frustration. The whole episode had been a disaster.

Angela looked at her in amazement. "What did you say? I don't know how you had the nerve to insult someone like that."

"He's just a man, and not a very nice one."

Robert's eyes narrowed thoughtfully. "I shouldn't have asked you to talk to him. Obviously your feelings about baseball are too deep to put aside."

Julie flinched at his sharp remark, but felt she had to defend herself. "I'm sorry that I let you down. But I honestly don't think there's anything I could have said that would have made him participate. His mind was made up before I ever opened my mouth. I didn't insult him until after he said no."

"I don't understand," Robert replied. "You're a wonderful, warm person. Everyone likes you. I've seen you exert incredible patience when dealing with some of our high-society patrons. I can't believe you would tell this guy off for no reason."

Julie just shook her head at the silent accusation. He could speculate all he wanted. There was no way she was going to tell them what had really happened between her and Matt Kingsley.

There was a long silence in the room, finally interrupted by the ringing of the telephone in the outer office. It was one of the board members calling for Robert.

He sighed when he heard the name. "The last thing I want to do is tell Emily Davenport that we failed on this," he said with irritation. "Her husband is a season ticket holder and one of their biggest fans."

"Maybe we can get some of the other Cougars," Angela suggested.

"Matt Kingsley *is* the Cougars. The rest of the guys look like amateurs next to him." He sighed again, sending them both a warning glance. "I haven't given up on Kingsley. There must be a way to change his mind. But in the meantime see who else you can get."

Julie nodded, taking a deep breath as he left the room.

Angela sat down in the chair next to her and offered her a commiserating smile. "We'll think of something."

"I really blew this one. I should have handled it better."

"Julie, I don't want to pry—"

"But you're going to, anyway," Julie finished with a wry smile. Angela was a good friend, but her degree in psychology always made her want to analyze emotions, and Julie was one of her favorite subjects, perhaps because she sensed the turmoil that lay just beneath her calm exterior.

"Not if you don't want me to." Angela sent her a quiet, disappointed look. "I just thought you might want to talk about your reaction to Matt Kingsley."

"I'd rather not. I just want to get back to work and try to figure out a way to make this cook-off a success without him."

"Okay. If you ever do want to talk—"

"I know, you're there." Julie pushed back her chair and stood up.

"What did he look like, anyway? Was he as handsome as his posters?"

"Better. I just wish he had more compassion, more sensitivity to go with the face." Her voice hardened. "But he doesn't care about helping people. The man has only one thing on his mind and that's baseball."

"Maybe that's why he's the best."

Julie shrugged. "More than likely. I think I'll call the Cougars again and see if any other players are available."

"I thought they weren't returning your calls."

"They weren't, but I have one more ace up my sleeve," Julie remarked, pulling a piece of paper out of her pocket.

"What's that?"

"Dale Howard's home phone number. I happened to see it on the Rolodex when the receptionist was writing down my message. I guess it's time to pull some strings.''

''Good luck.''

Julie walked slowly back to her office. She was sure Dale Howard would talk to her if she could just get him on the phone, and he certainly owed her a favor. As a little girl, she had shagged fly balls for him and her father for hours.

She sat down at her desk and dialed the number before she could change her mind. Unfortunately, the answering machine picked up the call, and she had no choice but to leave another message. Tired of spinning her wheels, she turned her attention to other projects. Finally, she got a return call from Dale just before five, and he promised to do what he could to sign up a few more of the players.

She worked into the evening, barely noticing when Angela stopped in to say goodbye. Julie was dedicated to her work at the foundation, and securing celebrities was only one small facet of her job. She was also responsible for coordinating the logistics of the events and handling publicity.

It was only when a knock came at her door that she realized the office had grown dark. She switched on her desk lamp, the light outlining a shadowy figure behind the glass panel. She was completely alone in the office. Her nerves tingled as the knock came again, and then the door slowly opened.

Chapter Two

"Julie Michaels." Matt Kingsley said her name with satisfaction, savoring her look of surprise.

Julie's hand dropped from the phone as she stared at him in amazement.

"What are you doing here?"

Matt walked farther into the room and moved a stack of folders off the chair so that he could sit down. "Do you mind?"

She shook her head bemusedly, watching him settle his large frame into a stiff armchair.

"It took me a while to track you down," he said conversationally, all trace of his earlier anger gone. "I couldn't remember the name of your organization, but your name stuck in my head. Then I asked up at the Cougars office if they knew anything about a cook-off, and they gave me this address."

She didn't know what to say. She was stunned that he had bothered to look for her after the way she had spoken to him.

Matt looked around her tiny office. It was typical of a small nonprofit organization. There were stacks of banners and posters in one corner, a desk overflowing with paperwork, and T-shirts from a recent walkathon piled on top of a filing cabinet.

"Looks like you're pretty busy."

"Why did you come here?" she asked again, fiddling with her ballpoint pen.

He stared at her, entranced by the way her golden hair caught the light from her desk lamp. She was even more beautiful than he remembered. But he couldn't tell her that. Instead he leaned forward and picked up one of the photographs on her desk, stalling for time.

"They look happy," he remarked.

Julie nodded as she looked at the group of smiling young faces. "They are happy, now. All of them were runaways at one time and most of them worked the streets. Now they're in school. Some are back with their families and some have found foster homes." She didn't know why she was telling him all that, but it seemed safer to talk about something neutral.

Matt set the photo down. He seemed suddenly unsure of himself and not at all like the overconfident man she had first encountered.

"Why did you come here?" she asked quietly. "I didn't think we had anything else to say to each other."

His lips curved into a twisted smile. "I wanted to apologize. Your response today shocked me, and it made me realize that I may have been a little insensitive."

She looked at him in amazement. It wasn't the greatest apology she had ever heard, but it was certainly surprising considering the source.

"I'm sorry, too. I had no right to yell at you. You certainly don't have to participate if you don't want to."

"But this event is really important to you."

"Not just to me, to a lot of people. I'd like you to understand." She dug into her desk drawer for their brochure and handed it to him. "Our foundation funds a great number of organizations up and down the state that deal in some way with children, and their emotional or physical health. The only way we can continue to operate some of these programs is through fund-raising. And the best way to raise money is with the help of celebrities. But I'm sure you already know that."

Matt nodded. He knew exactly what she was saying, and he could see her side; he just wished she could see his. Everyone wanted a piece of him. Sometimes he had to draw the line.

His smile broadened as she leaned down to dig out some more brochures. Her silky blouse was open at the throat revealing the shadowy cleft between her breasts, drawing his attention to the soft luminescence of her skin. On first appearance she seemed fragile, but he knew there was fire lurking just beneath the surface.

He should have stuck by his decision not to participate in their event. But he couldn't deny that Julie Michaels had made a deep impression on him. Her passion, not to mention her beauty, had been tormenting him all day. She didn't like baseball players. It was an impossible challenge to resist.

"These will give you an idea of the variety of programs we cover," she said professionally, placing a stack of folders before him. "But what they can't tell you about is the real people that benefit." She picked up the photograph again. "That's why I keep this here. I look into these young, hopeful faces and I try to remember how much they need us."

Julie's voice trailed off under his intent stare. His eyes seemed to burn right through her. "You probably don't want to hear about all this."

"You're wrong." His voice rang clearly through the office. And he was referring to much more than her last statement. "I do care about other things besides baseball."

"You do?"

"Yes. I'd like to explain something to you."

She shook her head. "You don't have to explain anything to me. I was way out of line. It's certainly your own business what you want to do." In fact, Julie didn't want to hear his reasons, because that might make him more human, more likable, and she was already having trouble keeping her guard up.

"I know I don't have to," he said in exasperation. "But give me a shot, okay?" He paused. "I flew in from New York yesterday, and I only got about three hours' sleep last night. Then at seven this morning I had a breakfast meeting with someone who wants me to plug their after-shave, and then another meeting with the head of the United Charities League, for which I am committed to providing at least three public-service announcements during baseball season. Then it was a quick lunch and off to batting practice. When you caught me afterward, I was exhausted. Otherwise, I wouldn't have responded the way I did. I'm not normally so rude. But the demands on my time are just getting ridiculous."

"That's because you're a star, and that wasn't another insult, just a fact."

He tipped his head in acknowledgment. "If you still want me, I'll participate in your event. Just tell me what I have to do."

"Really? You just said the demands on your time were incredible."

"They are. But I think I can squeeze this one event in."

"Why? What changed your mind?"

He laughed. "You. You're a fighter. I like that." A curious gleam entered his sparkling green eyes. "I have a feeling that there's more to you than meets the eye."

Julie didn't respond. It pleased her that he hadn't made the connection between her name and her father's, that he hadn't suddenly changed his mind because of that.

"So what do I have to do?" he inquired.

She stared at him for a moment, and then pointed to one of the flyers in his hand. "You just have to dig out a favorite recipe and enter it in the cook-off, which will be held at the Ambassador Hotel. You'll be one of the celebrity chefs and you'll have your own kitchen area in the ballroom to do your cooking. Then your entry will be judged along with the other celebrities." She paused as his mouth dropped open. "What's wrong?"

Matt looked at her in genuine dismay. "You didn't say I had to cook."

"Just something simple."

"I can't cook," he said flatly.

"Of course you can. Everybody can cook something."

He shook his head. "Not me. I eat out or I order in."

Julie sent him a suspicious look. Was this just another way for him to get out of the event? She wouldn't put it past his smiling face. The man had charm all right, more than she cared to admit, and for just a moment she had started to relax.

"If you don't want to do this, just say so."

"I do want to. But I can't cook. What do you suggest?"

"You really can't cook anything?" she asked finally.

"Is a tuna fish sandwich cooking?"

"No."

"Then I can't cook anything." He leaned back in his chair and propped his feet on the edge of the desk. He had changed his jeans for casual slacks and another sweater, but there was no mistaking the athletic build.

Julie blushed as her eyes met his in unmistakable awareness.

"Is there something else that I could do?" he asked deeply, his mind running along a different line than his words. "Sign autographs, pose for pictures?"

Or kiss me again, she thought outrageously, forcing her eyes away from his captivating smile.

"Of course there are other responsibilities, but you still need to cook. That's the focus of the event," she said crisply, trying to think of a solution. Maybe he could team up with another player, and they could make something together. Although that didn't really fit into the rules or the spirit of the event. The fans wanted to know what Matt Kingsley's favorite meal was, and for one hundred and fifty dollars a plate, they wanted to watch him cook it and then eat it with him.

"Do you cook?" Matt asked with a thoughtful look in his eyes.

"Of course."

"Then you can teach me."

His quiet statement shocked her, instantly bringing to mind images of them standing together in her kitchen, beating eggs, laughing and—

"No. No. I couldn't do that."

"Why not? All you have to do is give me a few lessons, and then I'll be ready."

"I don't know. I'm so busy with work."

"I thought this event was important to you," he challenged.

"It is."

He folded his arms on his chest. "It's your call."

Julie paused at the suddenly wicked glint in his eyes. He had her, and he knew it. But she was going to go down fighting. "All right. I'll give you one lesson. That's it."

"It's going to take more than one," he said wisely. "But it's a start. When?"

"Tomorrow."

"Tonight."

"It's nearly seven," she protested.

"I know, and I'm starved. It's a perfect time to start, unless you have other plans?"

"No, but we'll have to stop at the store and pick up a few things. I haven't had time to shop lately."

"What will you make?" he asked interestedly as she began to pile her work on the edge of the desk.

"I won't make anything. You will. I suppose you might as well learn how to cook your favorite food. That's what you'll need for the cook-off. What is it, anyway?"

"My favorite food?" he repeated with a grin.

She shook her head warningly. "If it's lobster, you're paying."

He laughed at her wary expression. "Hot dogs covered with homemade chili, hot enough to make you sweat, with grated cheese and onions dripped on top. A side of potato salad and hot apple pie with vanilla ice cream for dessert." He pinched his fingers together. "Voilà, the perfect meal."

She bit back a smile. "That's disgusting. It's unhealthy in just about every way imaginable. And you, an athlete, should know better."

"I grew up at the baseball park. What can I say? Hot dogs are in my soul." His grin faded at her suddenly tense expression. "Julie?"

She shook her head and picked up her purse. "Let's go. You can follow me. There's a supermarket about a block from my apartment."

"If you want something different, it's fine with me."

"No, hot dogs sound just fine." Every bite would remind her not to let him get too close. He was a baseball player. It didn't matter that he seemed nicer than she had first thought. First impressions were almost always deceptive, and she knew she couldn't trust him. It might be wrong to compare him with her father, but she couldn't help noticing the similarities, the overwhelming attractiveness, the fan adulation, the charm. She had let herself love once before. She wouldn't make that mistake again.

"Just put the bags on the counter," Julie instructed sharply as she unlocked the door to her apartment.

"Aye-aye, sir."

She made a face at his remark, although she knew he was only remarking on her less-than-friendly behavior. She had been acting like a drill sergeant all evening, and she knew it was silly, but it was the only way she could keep her distance.

More than once she had felt like laughing at his complete bewilderment in the supermarket. But that would have made their evening seem more like a date than a business arrangement. So instead she had retreated into icy politeness, trying to maintain an attitude of quiet, impersonal efficiency.

Matt set the bags down by the sink and groaned as he sank into one of the kitchen chairs. "This cooking stuff is exhausting."

"We haven't started the cooking yet," she reminded him, taking out a pan for the hot dogs. "And you're in charge. I give the instructions. You do the work."

"Yes, sir."

She sighed at his lazy grin. "I don't think you're taking me seriously."

His smile faded as he looked at the lovely, slender woman in front of him. She was a complicated mix of hot and cold, her attitude toward him changing with every minute. She was a challenge, and he never backed away from a challenge.

Deliberately, he got up from his chair and walked over to her.

Julie's body tensed at his approach. She was pushing him. She knew it, but she couldn't seem to stop herself. She tried to turn away, but he grasped her shoulders, holding her firmly in place.

"On the contrary," he said deeply. "I have some very serious thoughts about you." He put a hand under her chin and tilted her head back so that he could look into her gold-flecked eyes. He saw the sudden flash of desire, and his own body instinctively responded to the silent invitation. He leaned forward, feeling her tense under his loose embrace, and then he pulled away.

Julie stared at him in confusion as he began unpacking the groceries. "What are you doing?"

"Making dinner. You're supposed to be helping," he reminded.

"Why did you do that?"

"Do what?"

"You know, I don't like your attitude."

Matt set the pan on the burner with more force than necessary. "I'm not exactly thrilled with yours, either. You have a huge chip on your shoulder, and it's obvious you're itching for a fight. So go on. Tell me what you think of me."

He placed his hands on his waist and waited, all traces of his earlier humor completely gone.

Julie licked her lips and started to tremble. Everything he had said was true. She wanted to dislike him. He was a baseball player, and someone she could never trust. But it was suddenly more complicated, and his reading of the situation stung.

"Why are you here?" she asked.

"Cooking lessons, remember?"

"You seem a little more interested in flirting than cooking."

Matt tipped his head. "Sorry. I can't seem to help myself. I don't usually come on so strong. But there's something between us. I can feel it. I think you can, too." He leaned back against the counter, folding his arms in front of him. "Desire, intense, irrational desire."

"Don't be silly."

"You can try to deny it...."

"I don't have to try. There's nothing between us. That's a fact."

His eyes narrowed thoughtfully. "Why are you so dead set against me?"

"Because I hate baseball." The words burst out of her.

His eyebrows shot up in disbelief. "Nobody hates baseball. It's all-American."

"I do. I hate everything about it, from the home runs to the beanball wars."

Matt stared at her in amazement. It was inconceivable that she didn't like baseball, or didn't at least pretend to like it. No woman would ever have the nerve to admit something like that to him. But her words did little to dampen his growing interest. Instead, he found himself rising irresistibly to the challenge.

"Sit down," he commanded, pushing her into a chair. He sat down across from her and waited. Baseball had taught him to be patient and to analyze before taking a swing.

"Why don't you just leave?" she said in desperation. It would be the best thing for both of them.

"No, I think it's only fair I get a chance to defend my profession."

"There's nothing you can say. I've heard every excuse, every argument, every rationalization about the game. But I don't like it, I'm sorry."

"Why?"

"It just doesn't interest me."

"You're a very stubborn lady."

"Baseball made me that way." The words slipped out before she could stop them, and his eyes narrowed shrewdly.

"Why do you say that? Were you involved with a baseball player, a love affair that went bad?"

"You could say that."

"I'd rather hear you say it. In fact, I'd love it if you would tell me what happened, why you feel the way you do."

"No," she snapped, suddenly realizing the trap she had fallen into. She didn't want to confide in Matt Kingsley, a man she barely knew and someone who certainly wouldn't understand her feelings.

"Talk to me, Julie."

"Just let it be."

"You can't blame baseball for a bad love affair," he said, unwilling to drop the subject. "There are jerks in every profession, not just professional sports."

"I know that."

"Then don't you think you're being a little bit irrational?"

"No, I don't."

"Why did you come to me if you hate baseball?"

"Believe me it wasn't my first choice. But the foundation is important to me, and this event needs a superstar, like you. I couldn't let my personal feelings get in the way, and quite honestly, my boss wouldn't let me."

His intent stare made her uncomfortable, and restlessly she got to her feet.

Matt watched as she systematically began putting the groceries away and getting dinner started. "You really care about your job, don't you?"

Her tension eased as he changed the subject. "I love it. I really enjoy doing work that means something."

"Unlike hitting a little ball over a fence," he said dryly, returning to their original theme.

She sighed. "I shouldn't have said that. I didn't mean to be insulting."

Matt shrugged his shoulders, tilting the chair back on two legs. "Why not? It's what you think. That's what impressed me about you today—your honesty. I don't get to hear what people really think about me. They're too busy trying to get something out of me. You may not believe it, but I just want to play baseball. I'm not really interested in all the stuff that comes along with it."

Julie shook her head in disbelief. "That's easy to say when you're rich and famous."

"Maybe. I don't know. Sometimes I think I was happier playing in the minor leagues. There was more camaraderie down there, more caring. In the majors there's a lot more pressure, and the pressure doesn't end when you get there. It's constant. You're always looking over your shoulder, waiting for some younger, stronger, faster guy to take your spot. I'm twenty-nine, getting old for a baseball player."

"But you're the best on the team."

"I've been the best. I hope I will be again. But every year is different, every game is like going out there for the first time."

Julie turned on the water and started washing the vegetables for the salad. She didn't want to keep talking about baseball, but she found herself caught up in his words, the emotion in his voice. "I don't understand what keeps driving you," she muttered. "You're a great player, and even if it ended tomorrow, you would have had a great career."

"I guess baseball is an obsession with me," Matt remarked. "It's been in my blood since I was a little boy and my dad took me to Boston for a game at Fenway. I stood at the top of the stadium and looked down at the shiny green diamond and thought it was the most beautiful thing I had ever seen.''

Her hands stilled as his voice captured her imagination. And when Matt's eyes locked with hers, she knew she had revealed too much.

''You know what I mean, don't you?'' The deep timbres of his voice sent a shiver down her spine.

''No,'' she denied. ''I've never cared for diamonds, baseball or otherwise.''

''Liar. I saw it in your face.''

''Just let it be.''

''I don't think I want to. You intrigue me, Julie Michaels.''

''Why? Because I said I don't like baseball? I'm sure there are hundreds of women who feel the way I do.''

''Maybe, but very few that would actually admit that to a baseball player. That's like waving a red flag in front of a bull.''

She smiled nervously at the darkening gleam in his eyes. ''I didn't mean it to be a challenge.''

''Too late. It's already done. And I never walk away from a challenge.'' He reached out and tilted her chin up so that she was looking directly into his sexy green eyes.

Chapter Three

Her breath caught in her throat and instinctively she tensed, not sure what she wanted him to say or to do. The intimate silence was suddenly shattered as the colander fell through her hands and landed with a clatter against the countertop.

"I do not intend to be a challenge," she said hastily, backing away. "We're going to work together on a charity event. That's it."

Her denial brought a smile to his face. "That's true. But there's something between us. The minute I saw you I knew you were special."

She hesitated and then shook her head. "You did not. You thought I was a groupie, anxious for a kiss," she reminded him, busying her hands once again.

His lips curved into a teasing smile that she found far too endearing. It lent a hint of boyishness to his sexy face, and in some ways was more dangerous than his sophisticated charm.

"Only for a minute," he replied. "As soon as I kissed you I knew that—"

"Please, I don't want to hear a comparison of all the kisses you've had in your life. At least not before dinner. And speaking of dinner—" she pushed a head of lettuce toward him "—you can start cutting that up and getting the salad ready. Then we'll move on to the chili. No more flirting, no more baseball."

Matt chuckled at her ground rules. He hadn't had this much fun with a woman in years. With Julie there was no room for pretenses or phony behavior. He liked that. He just wished he could convince her there was another side to baseball.

Julie picked up the lettuce and tossed it to him. "Get to work. I'm hungry."

"Aye-aye, sir."

Julie smiled to herself. Apparently they had come full circle.

The rest of the evening passed in relative quiet. Their earlier conversation had cleared the air, and although there was still a shadow between them, they were able to behave more naturally with each other. Julie was basically an outgoing person as was Matt, and they found that once they started talking, they had quite a few things in common.

They dropped the topic of baseball and moved on to more neutral subjects like movies and books. They shared their opinions without hesitancy, enjoying the give-and-take of an honest, friendly conversation.

Under Julie's eagle eye the meal came out perfectly, and while it wasn't haute cuisine, she thought it would make an interesting entry to the cook-off. Not that she had a choice, Matt had a hard time just boiling the hot dogs. He hadn't even tried the chili, and she had been too hungry to prolong the cooking lesson.

When he left shortly after ten, Julie felt like a hurricane had blown through her apartment. It wasn't just the chaotic pile of pots and pans that made her feel that way; it was the unexplained ache somewhere in the region of her heart.

She busied herself with the cleaning so that she wouldn't have time to think about him. It didn't work. She kept remembering the way his lips curved into a teasing smile, the bright sparkle in his light green eyes, the tender softness in his voice when he had said goodnight. He hadn't kissed her, but she wished he had.

Julie got up the next morning feeling a tingle of excitement in her bones as she dressed for work. She hadn't slept much, but she didn't feel tired. She was looking forward to telling Robert and Angela the good news.

Her usual commute from her apartment in Noe Valley to the foundation offices on the wharf passed quickly. She didn't mind that the streets were crowded or that cars were continually double-parking in front of her, because inside she was feeling happy, unexplainedly happy. The sun seemed brighter to her, the tourists more cheerful, the other drivers more courteous.

She knew Matt was responsible, although she hated to admit that a man could have such an impact on her life. She had decided a long time ago that she didn't want to get involved in love or romance until she found the right man, someone who was trustworthy and stable, someone who would never leave her the way her father had. Matt certainly didn't fit into her strict criteria, but he was much nicer than she had expected, with a brand of charm that was irresistible.

She was still smiling about their dinner when she walked into her building. It was just past eight and the office was already buzzing with activity. She went about her usual routine, exchanging her suit coat for a comfortable sweater, checking the stack of early-morning messages and then it was time for coffee.

Angela was popping a pastry into her mouth when Julie walked into the back room. With a wide grin Julie grabbed her by the arm and headed for Robert's office.

"Where are we going?" Angela complained, trying to talk and chew at the same time.

"You'll see." Julie rapped on his door and poked her head in just as he set down the telephone.

Robert looked up in surprise as she dragged Angela into the room and pushed her toward a chair. He was used to informality in the office, but this was unusual.

"What's up?" he asked.

"That's what I'd like to know," Angela grumbled, straightening her skirt.

Julie laughed. "Do you remember when you told me you needed a man? A rich, handsome, famous man who could cook?"

"Are you sure you two don't want to do this alone?" Robert inquired, looking a little uncomfortable.

Angela stared at her in surprise. "Don't stop now."

"Matt Kingsley." Julie proclaimed his name as if he were a visiting king, and in a way he was.

Robert sat back in his chair, his eyes narrowing thoughtfully.

"Matt Kingsley is going to be in the cook-off," Julie added.

"Darn. I thought you were getting him for me," Angela complained good-naturedly. "How did you do it? I thought you told the poor guy off."

"I did. But as fate would have it, my outspokenness just made him more interested."

"A man who likes a challenge." Robert looked at her with a gleam in his eye. "Good job."

"I can't really take credit. I didn't intentionally send out a challenge. It just came out that way."

"So when did you see him? What did he say?" Angela asked.

"He came by the office late last night. He apologized for his earlier rudeness and said he would do the cook-off. There is one small problem, though."

"I knew it was too good to be true," Angela muttered.

"He can't cook."

Robert chuckled. "I don't care if he can cook. As long as he smiles, tells his friends to come and signs a few autographs, the man can burn his entire entry."

"He might just do that," Julie retorted.

"Maybe I should offer to teach him," Angela said thoughtfully.

Julie flushed with embarrassment. "Actually, he already asked me."

Angela smiled knowingly. "Now why didn't I figure that out?"

"I'd like to get him tied into some of our pre-event publicity, as well," Robert said briskly, getting back to business. "Of course we'll do the usual news release, but I wonder if we could get him to record the public-service announcements for the radio. That would make it much more personal, more exciting. And I'd love to set up a photo shoot with him and some of our other chefs at one of the Family Service Centers or even the local hospital."

"Hold on just a minute," Julie interjected. "I don't know how much time he has to commit to this. He said he would do the cook-off, but I don't know about the rest."

"Convince him," Robert said simply. "I'm sure you can do it. Now, ladies, if you'll excuse me, I have to make a phone call, and you two have about a hundred things to do."

"A thousand," Julie corrected. "But today I feel up to the challenge."

Angela laughed as she and Julie walked out to their offices. "I think I know why. And you don't need a degree in psychology to recognize—"

"Don't say it. I admit he's an exciting man, but there's nothing else going on."

"Tell me another one," Angela called after her as she scurried into her office and shut the door.

Julie smiled to herself, took out her list of things to do and started working.

She didn't hear from Matt for the next two days, and her excitement slowly faded away. Deep down she had expected him to call or come by. He was the one who had suggested there was something between them. But now he seemed to have completely lost interest. The thought was unusually depressing.

She hadn't called him about doing publicity. She was hesitant to push his friendliness, and despite her words to the contrary, she did understand the pressures of his position. But Robert was adamant about using him, so when the end of the week rolled around, and she still hadn't heard from him, she picked up the phone and called the Cougars.

Matt was unavailable. It was what she had expected. She didn't have his home number, so she would have to wait for him to get in touch with her, if he ever did. He had probably just been spinning her a line, and she was foolish enough to fall for it. There was certainly no reason why a man like him would be interested in someone like her.

By the end of the day she still hadn't heard from him, and with the weekend looming ahead, she felt somewhat discouraged as she drove home. She tried to think positively about her life. There were plenty of things she could do during the weekend that would be fun. She could take a walk through Golden Gate Park, take the ferry over to Sausalito or just laze around. She didn't need a man to make her life complete, although she was beginning to wonder if she shouldn't have accepted Angela's invitation for happy hour. At least she could have come home later with less time to moan about a lonely Friday night.

But it was too late now, and she decided to punish herself a little more by thinking about what Matt probably did with his weekends. It wasn't baseball season yet, and he was a single, very eligible bachelor, not to mention attractive, sexy. She sighed. He was probably hitting the night spots with a gorgeously thin model— someone who would look perfect sitting in his bright red Ferrari.

She smiled at her dismal thoughts. She was being ridiculous, and she wasn't used to feeling sorry for herself. It was silly. She had chosen to live the way she did. Her father was a wealthy man, and her mother was very well-off. She could have had the same life-style, but she didn't want it. What she had was infinitely more satisfying because it was all hers.

She pulled up in front of her garage—a precious piece of real estate that had added another hundred dollars to her rent. After opening the door, she hopped back into her car, pulled inside and then walked out and headed toward the front of her building. The evening air was damp and foggy as it hit her face, but she found it more invigorating than annoying.

After five years in San Francisco, she had actually gotten to like the fog that crept in every night, obliterating the sun and separating her tiny neighborhood from the rest of the city. With her head bent down to keep the moisture out of her eyes, she almost didn't see the bright red car. But the man leaning nonchalantly against the hood couldn't be missed.

"Hi," Matt said, walking over to join her.

"Hi." Her brown eyes sparkled with excitement, and she couldn't stop the warm smile that spread across her face.

Matt regarded her with quiet satisfaction. His imagination hadn't done her justice. The big dark eyes contrasted with hair the color of sunlight, and the sexy, soft body was noticeable even in a somber business suit. He hadn't been able to forget her, but it wasn't just for her beauty—it was the challenge in her eyes and the directness of her smile. He was tired of playing games with women, tired of being a star. Thank God he had finally found a woman who wasn't impressed by him.

Julie fidgeted under his intense gaze, wondering just what was going on behind that lazy smile. "What are you doing here?"

"You keep asking me that," he complained, feeling an inexplicable sense of relief at her welcome. He hadn't known what to expect with a woman as unpredictable as she was.

"That's because you keep showing up unexpectedly. Haven't you ever heard of a telephone?"

He grinned. "It doesn't have quite the same impact, and it's a lot easier for someone to say no when they can't see your face."

"Are you going to ask me something?"

"Inside," he replied, tipping his head toward her apartment. "I'm freezing."

"You should have waited in the car," she suggested, putting her key into the lock.

"I was afraid I'd miss you. The fog gets really thick here."

She nodded as he walked up the stairs with her. "It used to bother me, but not anymore. Where do you live?"

"Down on the peninsula. Foster City."

"It's nice there. Very modern, sophisticated. I understand quite a few professional athletes live there. It must be the ambience." She unlocked the door to her apartment and let him in. The room was chilly, and she immediately went over to turn on the heat.

"I'm afraid I haven't noticed much more than the endless stream of traffic from the stadium to my house. I've lived there for four years, but I usually spend the off-season down at my parents' house in San Diego. Damn, it's cold in here." Matt wrapped his arms around himself for warmth and then walked into the kitchen, making himself at home. He checked her refrigerator and her cupboards while she watched in amazement. He certainly wasn't one to stand on ceremony.

"The cupboard is bare," he said finally, leaning over her countertop with a disgusted sigh. "I thought you were a cook."

"I am. But I do work full-time, and sometimes it doesn't seem worth it to cook just for one."

"How about for two?" he suggested with a gleam in his eyes.

"You're the one who needs practice."

"I also need food. I'm starving."

"You said that last time. Don't you ever eat?"

"I burn it all off."

She laughed. "I don't think hitting a baseball burns off that many calories."

"I do a little more than just hit a ball. There's weight training and aerobics, long-distance runs, sprints. It's an exhausting job."

"Poor baby."

"Did anyone ever tell you that you're a tough woman?"

"I think tough broad was the term he used, but he was about fourteen and I had to sit him down and convince him that school was more than just a place to meet chicks."

"You are heartless." His smile took the edge off his statement. "But seriously, since there's no food here, and I'm hungry, and you're hungry, why don't we go out? I'm very good at ordering pizza."

Her stomach grumbled at the mention of food. She was hungry. "You've got a deal."

He looked surprised by her casual acceptance. "You're going out with a baseball player? Aren't you afraid I'll start quoting batting averages over the pepperoni?"

She made a face at his teasing comment. "I'm going to eat pizza with you, but—"

"What's the catch?"

"No baseball?" she asked hopefully.

"No way," Matt retorted. "I'm going to tell you my life story, and believe me it's filled with baseball."

She rolled her eyes, but inwardly she was pleased. She wanted to get to know him better, just for a night, just until the cook-off. Then he would fade out of her life and everything would be back to normal.

"Once upon a time there was a little boy growing up in the middle of a Kansas cornfield. He used to cut long branches from the trees to use as a bat, and every morning he would get up and practice hitting a ball, a very old, battered ball, at the big barn door," Matt said dramatically as they waited for their pizza to be made.

Julie took a sip of her wine, leaning back against the booth with a lazy smile. "A Kansas cornfield, huh?"

Matt tipped his head, a teasing gleam in his eyes. "Okay, it was San Diego, but that doesn't seem to have quite the impact."

"Especially since there aren't any cornfields there."

"You got me."

"What's the real story?"

"I warn you, it's a lot less exciting."

"I'll take my chances. Go on."

"I was born Matthew Lawrence Kingsley in San Diego, California, the oldest of three children, all boys. My mother was a hairdresser, my father was a general contractor. We had a nice, uneventful life, the usual childhood, teenage rebellions, but nothing extraordinary. And then there was baseball."

"Wait." Julie reached for the liter of wine and poured herself another glass. "I think I'm going to need this."

Matt shook his head in disgust. "It's not a bad word, you know."

"Go on with your story." She slowly sipped her wine, feeling only a little uncomfortable as he related the events of his childhood. It didn't hurt to hear him talk about baseball. They had shared many of the same feelings. It was only later when her father had betrayed them, that she had pushed aside all the good memories.

"My dad started taking me to baseball games when I was about three years old. And by the time I was seven I was in love with the game. I played all through school and one year of college. Then I got picked up by the L.A. Stars and about four years ago got traded to the Cougars. That's when I really found my stride. Dale Howard is one of the best managers in the league."

"He used to be a great player," Julie interjected.

"How do you know that?" he asked with interest.

"I do occasionally read the sports page. Go on with your story."

His eyes rested on her face for a long time, puzzled by the strange sadness in her eyes. "Let's talk about something else."

"No," she said quickly. "Please go on. What about your brothers? Are they ballplayers?"

"No, they played when we were growing up, but not anymore. Jimmy is the middle kid. He just finished law school and is getting ready to take the bar exam. Greg is the baby. He's twenty-two, a senior at San Diego State. I don't think he knows what he wants to do yet. Right now he spends a lot of time on the beach or at school picking up chicks."

"You sound like you're very fond of your brothers."

Matt nodded. "They're okay. We have a pretty close family, although my mom is dying for one of us to get married and bring a woman into the group. She's been outnumbered for years."

Julie smiled at the thought of a big, laughing family. It was something she had always longed for. "What does your mother think of your fame?"

"She still thinks I'm a smart-mouth kid who just happens to be able to hit a baseball better than most people. The two of you would probably get along very well."

"I'm sure she's proud of you."

"Yeah, but she would be proud of me no matter what I did. She's my mom."

Julie took another sip of wine. "Okay, go on, tell me about baseball and Matt Kingsley. Tell me why you play the game."

"Why? I have hundreds of reasons for playing. I love everything about it. I enjoy the competition, I like the athletics, the power, the strength and the challenges. I guess I'm just obsessed with being the best baseball player of all time," he said finally. "I can't explain the thrill I get from hitting the ball right on the sweet spot of the bat, watching it go over the fence. It's just an unexplainable high."

"You've never considered doing anything else?" she asked as a wistful note crept into her voice.

He shook his head. "Never. Baseball is a part of me. I can't imagine giving it up. I know I will one day, probably not too far from now. But I always want to be involved with the game in some way—helping other kids get started, coaching, whatever I can do."

Julie nodded. It was what she had expected. He was a ballplayer through and through. A hard knot settled in her stomach.

"So tell me about you," Matt suggested.

"There's not much to tell," she replied. "I'm an only child. My mother and father are divorced, and I live alone in San Francisco."

"I think you've skipped a few major points."

"My life is not really all that interesting."

"What are your parents like?"

"They're..." She hesitated. She had never really lied about her parents before. Both Angela and Robert knew about her background, but telling Matt would create an intimacy between them, a bond that she wasn't sure she could handle. She didn't trust herself to get too close to him.

"Are they still alive?" Matt asked, breaking into her thoughts.

"Yes, they're alive. We get together now and then, but my work keeps me pretty busy."

He let her vagueness pass with a wry twist of his lips. "What about the rest of your life? Any hobbies, any passions—any men?"

She flushed under his intent stare. "That's a rather personal question."

"That's not an answer."

"My hobby is my work. I don't have much time for anything else. Nonprofit organizations are notoriously understaffed, and ours is no different."

"You didn't answer the rest of my question," he persisted. "Is there anyone else in your life?"

"Why are you so interested?" she countered, her finger running nervously around the edge of her wineglass.

"Because I'm interested in you."

"Even though I don't like baseball?"

He tilted his head. "I'm hoping I can change your mind."

"Is that why you asked me to dinner tonight—to change my mind?"

"Maybe I just want to get to know you better. After all, we'll be working together in the future."

"That's hardly a reason to become best friends," she said.

"You don't like to talk about yourself, do you?"

"I'd much rather hear about you. Any women in your life?" she asked brightly.

"No one serious. Like you, I don't have much time to form deep relationships."

"Of course you don't," she muttered.

"What did you say?"

She shook her head. "I'm sure there must be a lot of women who want to go out with you."

He shrugged his shoulders. "A lot of women like the idea of going out with a ballplayer. But I'm not sure the reality always lives up to their expectations."

Her eyes widened at the honesty in his simple statement. Was he really this humble, or was it just an act for her benefit? "What do you mean by that?"

"Baseball players are just normal guys who happen to make a living in the public spotlight." He leaned forward, resting his arms on the table and studying the mixed emotions flitting through her eyes. "You don't believe me, do you?"

"I don't know what to believe. You're different than I expected."

"So are you," he countered softly. "I think we should get to know each other better, don't you?"

Julie felt a chill run through her bones. He was so serious all of a sudden, so intense, and when she looked into his eyes, she saw unmistakable desire. Their glances locked, and in that long moment she made her decision.

Chapter Four

"Yes," she whispered so softly that he had to lean forward to hear her. "Yes."

He stared at her thoughtfully, his eyes noting the fire in her cheeks, the wariness in her eyes, the nervous drumming of her long slender fingers against the red-checkered tablecloth.

"Aren't you going to say anything?" she asked quietly, unnerved by his long silence. Perhaps she had misread the situation, taken the look of desire in his eyes too seriously.

"Yes," he said finally, echoing her earlier statement. "I think we should get to know each other." He reached across the table for her hand, his touch setting off another fire in her soul. "That means you have to open up a little, tell me things about yourself that you never tell anyone else."

"Like what?" she inquired nervously.

He smiled then, releasing the tension with his teasing eyes. "Like whether or not you like onions on your pizza."

She sat back in her seat and shook her head. "I don't."

"Or if you read the comics before the sports section."

"I read everything before the sports section," she said lightly.

"What time you get up in the morning and what time you go to bed," he added, with a devilish gleam in his eyes.

"I'll never tell. There are some things that were meant to be private."

They looked at each other and laughed at the same time, and then laughed again at the coincidence. Julie couldn't remember a time when she had felt so happy, so in tune with another person. She wasn't going to worry about the future, about baseball games or cook-offs, she was just going to enjoy the evening, the romance and every last bite of pizza.

It wasn't until they were walking up the steps to her apartment that Julie remembered her earlier phone call, and reluctantly she forced herself to bring up the subject of work.

"Do you want to come in for a few minutes?" she asked, pausing in front of her door.

Matt looked at her in surprise. "Really?"

"Business. We need to talk business," she said hastily, opening the door and flooding the apartment with light.

"What business is that?"

"The cook-off."

"Whatever you want me to do." He took a seat on the sofa, leaning back with a relaxed sigh. "But I think we better stick with the hot dogs and chili, unless you have time for about a hundred more cooking lessons in the next six weeks."

"Unfortunately not," she replied with a small smile, deliberately taking a seat on the chair across from him. Her apartment was suddenly too cosy, too intimate. "It's about publicity. We need your name, your support in the advance publicity for the cook-off."

He nodded warily. "Okay. Why don't you give me an idea just what that involves."

She shook her head at his worried expression. "I'm sorry, Matt. I hate to ask you for more time, when I know how busy you are. But this is my job."

"You don't have to apologize. I'm not going to hold it against you."

"Thank you." She paused. "Basically, we want to use your name on all media and print materials which include press releases, radio announcements, flyers, tickets and human-interest stories."

"That sounds easy enough. You can throw my name around as much as you like. Is that it?"

"We'd like to actually use your voice for the radio spots, if you have time to make the recording. We'd also like to book you for some interviews on the local radio and television talk shows." Her voice trailed off as his smile faded.

Abruptly he stood up, and walked restlessly over to the window, his eyes seeking understanding from the distant lights of downtown. He didn't want to upset their tenuous truce, but he had to say no. He had to keep his priorities straight.

"Matt? Did I say something wrong?"

He shook his head and then turned back around to face her gently enquiring gaze. "No, you're just doing your job. Unfortunately I have to do mine. I can't devote the kind of time you're talking about to the cook-off. The season is just around the corner. I have to practice, increase my training sessions, get mentally focused. We leave for Phoenix the week after your event."

"I understand," she said briskly. "Don't give it another thought."

"You don't understand. I want to help when I can, but I can't commit to a whole series of events."

"It's all right. You don't have to explain."

"Why don't we start with the radio announcements and see what else I have time for?"

She felt a prick of guilt at the weariness in his voice, and she knew she wasn't being fair. "I'm sorry, Matt. I don't want to push you into anything. My boss has been pressuring me, and understandably so, since you're the most popular celebrity we have. The radio spots would be wonderful, but only if you really feel you have time to do them. Otherwise, we'll find someone else."

"I'll do them. I want to help you."

She nodded her head. There was no mistaking his sincerity. "Thank you."

He returned her smile with a lazy grin. "Now that we've finished business—"

"You'll probably have to be going," she said deliberately.

"But when am I going to see you again?"

"You mean to do the radio announcements?"

"No, to see you. To prove to you that baseball players can be wonderful human beings even if some of us can't cook. What about tomorrow night? Do you have plans?"

"Tomorrow?"

"Yes, Saturday night. I suppose you already have a date?"

She smiled at the curious sparkle in his green eyes. "No, I don't have a date."

"Why not?"

"Nobody asked," she said simply, honestly. "What about you?"

"Nobody asked." He offered her a disarming grin. "So I'm asking you."

She shook her head. "Actually I can't. I promised Angela I would supervise our volunteer mail-stuffing session tomorrow. It starts at four and usually goes until about eight. We order out for dinner and stay until everything is done."

"What exactly are you stuffing?"

"Our quarterly newsletter. We can't afford a mailing house, so a couple of our volunteers come in and help. We can get everything done in a few hours, and the price is right."

"Can anyone help, or does this require special training?"

"Why?" she asked suspiciously.

"Because I want to volunteer."

"Why would you want to do that? You just got finished telling me that every spare second is filled with baseball."

"Okay, I exaggerated a little bit. I do have some free time in the evenings."

"And you want to stuff envelopes?" she asked in disbelief.

"Not particularly, but since that's what you're going to be doing, I figure it could be interesting."

She hesitated, flattered by his persistence in wanting to get to know her, but still suspicious of his motives. Matt Kingsley would have no trouble finding a woman to take out for the evening. Why her? Was he truly interested in her or did she just represent a challenge—a woman who didn't like baseball players?

"Say yes, Julie," he commanded. "Don't think about it. Don't try to find an excuse. Just say yes."

She looked up at the ceiling for a moment, realizing how vulnerable she was. He was too charming, and he had all the right answers.

"I give up. You can come, but I don't think you're going to enjoy yourself. You could probably better use the time, working on your batting stance or whatever it is ace hitters do."

"I probably could," he admitted. "But I think I can give up a Saturday night for a good cause, and I'm not talking about the foundation," he added, his gaze resting for a long moment on her flushed cheeks, the gently swelling curve of her lips, the glitter of gold in her eyes. He wanted. Lord, he wanted. But he turned away and walked deliberately out the door.

Newsletter stuffing was not ordinarily a task Julie found particularly invigorating despite her dedication to the job. The only good thing about it was that it gave her a chance to talk to the volunteers in a casual, personal setting, and tonight's group was one of her favorites—five teenagers who had all been helped in some way by their programs. She smiled as she looked around the long conference table and saw each volunteer folding, stuffing or stamping, and each face trained on Matt's tousled brown hair as he busily attacked his own stack of work.

The kids had been stunned when Matt had walked into the office in his faded blue jeans and wool sweater. The boys had been awed by his presence and the girls smitten by his looks. It had taken them nearly an hour to settle down enough to get back to the business at hand.

The running conversation at the table was baseball, of course, and in some ways it was an evening of torture for her, because their innocent conversation dredged up memories of the past when she and her father would argue for hours about the best hitters, the sliest pitchers and the craftiest base runners.

But this conversation took a much different twist than the ones she remembered. Where her father had always reigned supreme in his opinions, Matt was open and friendly. He listened, added his own comments and complimented them on their amateur insights. He was nice, he was caring, he was everything a hero should be, at least on the outside.

She just wished she could believe as easily as the kids did. But she had been fooled before, and she just couldn't forget that.

The evening flew by as they continued working over several cartons of Chinese food. They managed to finish the mailing just before eight o'clock.

"That's the last one," Anthony announced, pushing his pile to one side. "Thank God."

Julie laughed at his disgusted expression. The others had already finished and left, and she and Matt were filling the mail cartons in preparation for shipping. "Just be grateful we only have to do this four times a year."

"I am. I am." Anthony got up and stretched, then shrugged his shoulders into his worn high school letterman's jacket. "It was nice to meet you," he said to Matt. "I still can't believe a guy like you would be sitting here stuffing envelopes with us. It doesn't go with your image, man."

"I like the company," Matt explained, sending Julie a pointed look.

Anthony followed his gaze and nodded knowingly. "I figured it was something like that."

"Matt, tell him why you're really here," Julie commanded, embarrassed by their matching grins.

Matt just raised his eyebrows.

"He's going to help in the cook-off, and he's trying to make me believe that baseball players are nice, sensitive men."

"Well, of course they are," Anthony said in amazement. "A lot of great guys play baseball."

"Listen to him, Julie. He makes sense," Matt advised.

Anthony looked from one to the other with all the wisdom of his seventeen years. "I think you two should go for it. He's a lot better than that Jim guy who always hangs around you."

Matt's eyes lit up at this interesting piece of information. "Jim?"

"A friend and a long-time supporter of the foundation," she explained.

"Really? Why didn't you mention him before?"

"Because it wasn't important. Do you need a ride home, Anthony?"

"No. I have my mom's car."

"I'll leave the tickets with Julie," Matt added as Anthony waved goodbye. "I promised them tickets to a game," he explained.

"Recruiting a few more fans?"

"It's no big deal. I have an allotment of tickets for every home game. I think they would enjoy it."

"I'm sure they would."

"They're a good bunch of kids. Anthony told me that he first met you at one of the family shelters down by Hunters Point. He said you were volunteering down there."

She nodded. "Yes, sometimes I help out at some of our agencies. It gives me a chance to make sure that the foundation is really giving support in the areas that need it the most. I spent a long time with Anthony and his mother. They've suffered a lot in the last few years. But things have turned around now. Anthony is finishing up high school, his mother has a job and his father has thankfully left the area."

"Abusive?"

"Very. But hopefully that's over, at least for them."

"You really care about them, don't you?"

She shrugged her shoulders, trying not to show how deeply she appreciated the compliment. "It's not hard to care. They're nice people. They deserve better." She pushed the last carton of newsletters against the wall and straightened up, rolling her neck back and forth to ease the sudden cramping of her muscles.

"You work too hard," Matt said thoughtfully. "Let me help you."

Before she could move, he had walked around behind her, placed his large hands on her shoulders and started to massage her tired muscles.

It was tempting to linger for just a moment. With her back to him, she couldn't see his face; she could only feel the calluses on his hands as he gently rubbed the bare skin around her neck, slipping under her hair to work on the knotted muscles. His touch was skillfully persuasive, forcing her to relax despite the tingling of nerves down her spine.

She closed her eyes for a moment, letting herself settle back against his hard chest. It wasn't until his breath gently fanned her neck and his hands turned her around to face him, that she realized she had let him get too close.

Looking into his serious eyes, she felt the tension return. She braced her hands against his chest in an attempt to keep her distance, but her traitorous body was suddenly filled with a desire to touch, to stroke the taut muscles beneath his shirt, to feel the power in his arms, the strength in his embrace.

"It's not enough," he whispered, tightening his arms around her until her face was buried in the curve of his shoulder.

The rough wool of his sweater against her cheek was endearingly masculine. The arms around her body were as strong and as comforting as she had known they would be. But she could tell Matt was not content with their embrace. With a groan, he raised her face, looking at her with an intensity that could not be denied. He kissed her, bringing his lips down to hers with a hunger that she realized had been building since their first meeting.

. Julie responded in kind, welcoming his lips, his tongue, his demanding mouth with a hunger of her own. It wasn't enough. She pressed herself closer, letting her hands roam over his chest, around his waist, and underneath his sweater. She pulled his shirt out from under the waistband of his jeans, eager to touch his skin, to get even closer to the heat that was burning between them.

Matt groaned at her touch, his mouth seeking her lips again and again until she was completely breathless. Finally, he pulled away. "Do you know what you're doing to me?" he demanded, his eyes turning jade with desire.

"The same thing you're doing to me," she whispered breathlessly, pulling away from him. She turned her back on him, afraid to see the expression on his face, and unwilling to have him see hers. With a shaky hand, she concentrated on cleaning up the conference table.

Matt watched her silently. He was still reeling from their kiss. He couldn't remember ever feeling an attraction so strong, so intense.

"I guess that's it," Julie said finally, pushing the roll of stamps back into the drawer. "We can go."

Matt nodded and handed over her purse and coat. She took them from him gratefully and they walked quietly out to the street where the foundation reserved two parking spaces. Matt's red Ferrari was parked right next to Julie's light blue Honda, and she couldn't help thinking that the two cars reflected their completely opposite personalities—one exciting and bold, one practical and reserved. For a moment, she was tempted to ask him to switch.

"Why don't we get a drink somewhere," Matt suggested as they paused next to her car. "There's a restaurant-bar around the corner, O'Leary's. Have you been there?"

"Yes, many times. It's very nice, relaxing."

"Sounds good to me. What about you?" He reached out and took her hand, reading the hesitation on her face. "No baseball. I promise."

She smiled. "You're on. An Irish coffee sounds perfect to me."

"My favorite drink. I knew we had something in common," he said with satisfaction, as they strolled down the block.

The streets lining Fisherman's Wharf were filled with tourists and natives enjoying the unusually warm evening. The fog was absent, and the stars sparkled brightly overhead as they walked along the street, content to just soak up the holiday atmosphere.

O'Leary's, with its view of the bay, was crowded as usual, but Matt's face brought instant recognition to the excited hostess who literally pulled a table out of the air. They were seated just off to the side, but attention was almost immediate. Two boys rushed over to get an autograph, followed by a few more families. It was nearly fifteen minutes before Julie and Matt were once again alone, and the silence that fell between them was distinctly awkward.

"I'm sorry about that," he said after a moment.

"It's all right. It's not your fault you're a star." She took a sip of her Irish coffee.

"Sometimes it happens. Sometimes it doesn't. The other night when we went out for pizza, no one came over, but tonight..."

"It's okay. I understand."

He studied her bent head with puzzled eyes. "Can you tell me about it, Julie?"

She looked up at him in surprise. "What do you mean?"

"Tell me about the man who left you with such a bad impression of baseball players."

She hesitated, afraid to let him see too much, but wanting him to understand that she wasn't just being judgmental, that she had good reasons.

"You can trust me," he added persuasively. "I want to know what I'm up against."

"My father," she said quietly, her eyes never leaving his face. "Jack Michaels."

He let out a silent whistle. "Jack Michaels is your father? He's one of the greatest players of all time and one of the best coaches in the league. I must have seen him play hundreds of times."

She saw the admiration in his eyes, and her voice grew cold. "So did I, only I think it was thousands, not hundreds."

Matt shook his head in amazement. "How can you be his daughter and hate baseball? I don't get it. His pitching was pure magic. His curve ball sat down the best hitters in the game. Damn, I wish I could have played with him," he muttered to himself. Julie's silence finally made him look up. Her face was pale and she was nervously running her gold chain through her fingers. "I don't understand."

Julie sighed. Reluctantly she tried to put her feelings into words. She would tell him just enough to keep him from probing any deeper. "It's because I am his daughter. I saw everything. I grew up following his spotlight and wanting to share it, but there wasn't room for a wife and a child, only baseball. He never had time for me or my mother."

She couldn't stop the bitterness from creeping into her voice. "His career came first and his fans came second. We were a distant third, if that. In the beginning we were happy with having just a small part of him, because we were so proud of his achievements. We knew that someday he would come back to us. But he didn't. He left, walked out. And there was no fanfare then, no one challenging his reasons, questioning his integrity.''

''Maybe no one knew,'' he said halfheartedly.

She shot him a shrewd look. ''They knew. Everyone knew. But they didn't want to tarnish the image. I can understand it, but it still hurts, because it meant that a man's batting average was more important than the way he treated his wife and child, as if a star baseball player didn't have a responsibility to be a good person.''

''Wait, slow down. You're blaming baseball for everything that happened.''

''That makes me sound silly and irrational,'' she said defensively. ''But yes, I do think that baseball made him the way he was. The sport turned him from an ordinary man into a god. He was every child's hero, and he loved the attention, the money, the fame. Why should he settle for one wife and one daughter when there were thousands of people out there who wanted to be with him?''

Matt shook his head back and forth, searching for the right words. He knew exactly what she was talking about. He had seen it happen. The attention, the applause was an incredible high. Ordinary men became immortal with one swing of the bat. He loved the thrill as much as anyone. It was part of his obsession for the game. He would be lying if he said it didn't matter.

''It doesn't have to be that way,'' he said finally. ''Baseball might have contributed to your father's problems, but it didn't make him do the things he did. I can't begin to say why he left your mother. Maybe there were problems you didn't even know about. You were a child.''

"I was seventeen, and I saw what was going on. I know what kind of man he was. His ego was much bigger than his heart."

"And all baseball players are tarnished with the same brush," he said flatly. "That's like blaming all women for Eve feeding Adam the apple."

"We are blamed for that," she said forcefully. "The woman is always seen as the temptress. I heard my father and mother arguing once, and he told her that it wasn't his fault, that those women made him sleep with them. Made him. We're talking about a six foot, two-hundred-pound athlete in superb condition." She shook her head in disgust.

Matt repressed a smile. It did sound ludicrous, but Julie didn't know how aggressive some women could be. He had nearly lost all his clothes one hot night in Chicago when the fans had mobbed him outside the stadium. But she was right. Her father could have said no.

"I'm not your father."

She flushed under his scrutiny. "Of course you're not."

"But you think of us in the same way."

"I'm trying not to think of you at all. I'm very grateful for your participation in the cook-off. I don't think we need to bring any kind of a personal relationship into this."

He waved her weak excuse aside. "Tell me more about your life back then, Julie. I want to understand what it was like through your eyes, the way you saw things."

Julie didn't want to answer, didn't want to get into the past, but Matt's direct, uncompromising stare made her realize how determined he was to know what had happened.

"My father was a star, a legend. He was followed, everywhere we went. When I was a small child, I didn't mind. I was very proud of him, and I was thrilled to be sitting next to him, to be his little girl. That made me special. The other kids would have given anything to have a dad like Jack Michaels."

"Was he a good father?"

Julie stared down at the swirling black liquid in her cup. Was he a good father? She wasn't sure she knew how to answer that question. "In a way, yes. He gave me a lot of material things. I never wanted for anything in that way. And he was kind when he was home. But he wasn't home very often, and that's really what bothered me the most." She paused for a moment, reflecting on the past.

"I could understand it during baseball season, but in the off-season he used to go fishing with his buddies. They'd go off for a week at a time, down to Mexico or wherever to go deep-sea fishing. I think he was really more comfortable just being with other men, with his friends. He really didn't want to spend a lot of time with his family, with me. That's what hurt the most."

"What about your mother? Was she lonely when he was gone?" he asked curiously, wondering about the two people who had left her filled with distrust.

"She was very lonely. I didn't notice in the beginning because I was too young. But by the time I went into high school, I knew something was wrong. And there were rumors, lots and lots of rumors about other women, all-night parties when the team was on the road. My mother must have known something was wrong, but she always defended him, praised him. She really loved him."

"She was a model or an actress, wasn't she? I'm sure I must have read something about her. Her name was Kathleen—"

"Kathleen Abbott. She was very beautiful, still is as a matter of fact. She has blond hair, blue eyes, tall, thin, legs that go on forever. She and my father made quite a pair together," she said softly. "But it was just an illusion."

"An illusion that lasted—how long? Seventeen years?"

"And nine months. I think I was conceived on their honeymoon."

"There must have been something between them to last that long."

Julie stared at him in confusion. "I suppose there was. What's your point?"

Matt chose his words carefully. "You said that baseball broke up their marriage, but I wonder if that's really true. I don't think a man's profession can break up his marriage unless there are other problems in the relationship. Your parents were together for seventeen years of baseball. If the sport was going to break them up, I think it would have happened a lot sooner."

"No, because as my father's career got better and better his marriage got worse. There was a direct correlation between how well he was swinging the bat and how much time he spent at home. When he was hot, he was gone. When he was cold as ice, that's when we saw him. We were the devoted, loyal family that loved him no matter what his batting average was, and he turned on us, he betrayed us."

Matt stared at her for a long moment and then shook his head. "I'm sorry."

"You don't have to be. It's not your fault."

"I wish you believed that."

"I do."

"Where is your mother now?"

"She lives in Vancouver. She got remarried last year. His name is Larry Jacobson, and he doesn't know a thing about baseball. I couldn't be happier for her."

Matt stared thoughtfully at her. "It sounds like your mother finally got rid of the past."

"Yes, I guess she did."

"So what about you?" He paused for a long moment. "Are you ever going to be able to forgive baseball for ruining your life?"

Chapter Five

She nodded her head. "I'm doing it, slowly perhaps, but it is happening," she admitted. "I'm here with you, aren't I?"

His mouth curved into a smile. "What about baseball?"

She shook her head warningly. "You promised no baseball."

"Humor me."

She sighed impatiently. She had already told him more than she wanted to. "What else do you want to know? I told you about my father and my mother. There really isn't anything else. I was an only child."

"Baseball. I want to know about you and baseball," he said intently, leaning forward on his elbows to look into her wary brown eyes. "I'm sure there was a time when you liked it, when you were interested in it. I can't believe you've always disliked the game."

"No. There was a time when I knew every player's batting average in the National League. I could recite pitcher stats and even mimic the signs of the team my father was playing for at the time."

"You could probably teach me a thing or two."

"I probably could have then. I played the game, too, and in those days there weren't that many girls playing baseball and very few organized leagues. I actually played on the boys' team in junior high school. I was the best hitter they had. It must have been in my genes or something," she said wryly. "I used to love the game, idolized the players like everyone else, until I learned the truth."

"What truth?" Matt asked sharply. "What didn't you know?"

"I didn't know what baseball players were really like," she said simply. "They were always nice to me. I was Jack Michaels's kid. I was even an honorary bat girl one night. His teammates were my uncles. I adored them."

"And they all let you down? Every single one of them? Wasn't there one good man in the bunch?"

She bristled under his attack. "There might have been. I don't know. Because what I found out about my father shocked me to the core." Her voice rose sharply as the memories flooded back.

"What happened, Julie?"

"I don't want to talk about it anymore. Okay?"

Matt swore under his breath, reaching out to dab the tear on her cheek with the corner of his napkin. He wished he could wipe the pain away as easily, but it was too deep. "Okay."

She stared at him and then turned away. "It's in the past now."

Matt shook his head. "But it's not. That's the problem. You have to come to terms with what happened, so that you can finally be free of it. Have you ever talked to your father about it?"

"No. I haven't seen him since the day he walked out."

"But you were only seventeen," he said incredulously. "Didn't he want to know how you were doing?"

"My mother and I moved out of Los Angeles, and came up here to San Francisco. We made a new home, new friends. My mother's parents live in Sonoma. I think he came by a few times but I wasn't at home. He wrote me some letters, but I never opened them. I was too angry, too upset. Every now and then he calls my grandparents to find out how I'm doing, but I really don't want to talk to him."

"But now that you're older and so much time has passed, aren't you a little curious to hear his side of the story?" Matt persisted.

"No. What could the man possibly say?"

"I have no idea, but somehow it seems important that you talk to him. Maybe he could tell you something you don't already know."

"I don't think so." She dropped her gaze, unwilling for him to see the pain. There was still a final piece of the puzzle to tell him. But she couldn't do it, not yet. She cleared her throat. "It doesn't matter anymore. Now that is absolutely the last thing I want to say about my father. It's your turn."

"My turn?"

"Yes. Tell me about your wonderful, loving family."

"That should bore you in about five minutes."

"No. I'd like to hear more about them. I like the way you look when you talk about your mother."

He cleared his throat uncomfortably, and she smiled, happy to put him on the hot seat for a change.

"I'm not sure I should ask—but how do I look?"

She contemplated the question. "Tender. Your eyes turn dark, softer, and you can't seem to talk about your family without a smile on your face. In fact, sometimes you're downright sensitive—for a jock." She flushed at her own words and the perceptive light in his green eyes.

"Thanks, I think."

"So go on, tell me about them."

"We're very ordinary, Julie. In fact, we're pretty dull. My mom and dad are both homebodies. My dad likes to work on our house, which is in a perpetual state of remodel, and my mom likes to garden when the weather is nice. The kids are gone now, so it's just the two of them at home, except when I barge in during the off-season or when my little brother has summer vacation."

"I'm sure they like to see you."

"They do, but they're probably just as glad to see us go. I think they're enjoying having the house to themselves."

"It sounds nice," she said wistfully. "I like ordinary families. Two parents who go to work and come home and a family of kids sitting around the dinner table, arguing, talking about their days. I think that sounds like heaven. When I was a little girl, I used to imagine that I had at least three brothers and three sisters. I would make up names for them and pretend that we shared our problems and laughed together. I guess all kids fantasize about what they don't have. You probably wished your brothers would disappear."

"At least three times a day," he admitted. "But now that we're grown up I kind of like having them around."

They both fell silent, listening idly to the chatter emanating from the tables around them. Finally, Julie spoke. "I'm glad we came here."

"So am I."

"It was nice of you to help out tonight. The kids loved having you there."

"What about you?"

She smiled softly. "I liked it, too." She finished her coffee and pushed her cup away. "I guess we should go. It's getting late."

He nodded and got to his feet, smiling goodbyes as people called out to him. Julie made her way swiftly through the restaurant, feeling uncomfortable with the attention. She was grateful when she pushed open the door and found relative quiet in the night air. Matt joined her within a minute, but she found it difficult to meet his inquiring gaze, so she turned and started walking back toward the office.

"Politicians get the same treatment, you know," Matt said idly, "as well as actors, singers, writers, television personalities and movie stars. There are a lot of people besides baseball players that suffer the spotlight of fame."

"Jim doesn't." The comparison came out before she could stop it, although the thought had been simmering in her mind ever since she had met Matt.

Matt's lips tightened. "Jim, the boyfriend?"

"I haven't had a boyfriend since I was sixteen. I hardly think the term applies anymore."

"How about lover, companion, significant other?"

Julie sighed, wishing she had never mentioned his name. "Just a friend. I only mentioned him because you're so determined to make me believe that at some time in my life I am going to have to come to terms with fame and notoriety and perhaps even live through it again. But that's not true. There are people who will never have their name written in the newspaper. Jim is one of them. He's a nice guy. He goes to work at a normal job, he has evenings and weekends off. He makes good money, but he'll never be rich. He'll probably make an excellent husband and father.''

''I can see you've thought a lot about it,'' Matt said, stopping so suddenly, she walked into him. He reached out a hand to steady her and then pulled her under the overhang of a closed building. He folded his arms around her, his eyes daring her to move away. ''Sounds like Jimbo is the perfect man for you.''

''For any woman,'' she replied, trying to pull away from his embrace.

''But especially for you.''

She stiffened at the anger in his voice. ''What do you want me to say?''

''I want you to answer one simple question.''

She didn't trust the look in his eyes or the way his arms tightened around her. ''What's the question?''

''Does he kiss you like this?''

Julie watched in fascination as his mouth came down to claim hers. There was plenty of time to pull away, but she couldn't move, and then his lips were on hers, taunting, tantalizing, making her forget everything but his taste and his touch. Finally, he pulled away, shoving his hands ruthlessly into his pockets.

''Do you want my answer now?'' she asked quietly.

''No, I don't think so.''

''Good night, Matt.'' She took a step and paused as his hand came down on her shoulder.

"Julie. Tell me."

She hesitated for a long contemplative moment, al-though there was really nothing to think about. "He never kissed me like that, and I never wanted him to. Good night." She turned and walked away.

"Telephone call, Julie. Line three," Angela's voice rang over the intercom.

"I'm busy. Who is it?"

"Our hero."

Julie smiled and reached for the phone. "Julie Michaels."

"Hello, Julie Michaels. How are you today?" Matt's voice filled the empty spot in her heart. She had spent a very long, lonely Sunday, wondering whether she was crazy for wanting to see him or a fool for trying to push him away.

"I'm fine. Busy though."

"I know what you mean, but we have some unfinished business."

"What's that?"

"My cooking lessons."

She hesitated. It was silly to continue seeing him, and his cooking wasn't really that important. As Robert had said, the guests would be too busy looking at him and talking with him to care whether or not he could cook haute cuisine.

"Are you still there?"

"Sorry, I was just checking my calendar."

"How about tonight?"

The blank page stared her in the face. "No, not to-night."

"Tomorrow, Wednesday, Thursday? You owe me one, Julie."

"I do not."

"I don't think your boss would agree with you."

He was right about that. Robert would be furious. Keep the celebrities happy. She swore under her breath. "Tomorrow will be fine. But I refuse to eat hot dogs again. We'll try something else, something simple."

"How about steak?"

"It figures you would be a meat eater."

Matt chuckled. "I like quiche, too. Whatever you want. You pick the menu. Just tell me what time."

"Seven o'clock."

"I'll see you then." He paused. "Oh, Julie, don't buy anything for dessert."

"Why?"

"You'll see. Goodbye."

The dial tone hummed in her ear and she set down the phone, refusing to acknowledge the lighthearted feeling that had crept into her soul. He was a charmer all right. If only he could cook.

But he couldn't cook, and one lesson turned into two and then three. They both knew it was hopeless and that the lessons were really no more than a sham for getting to know one another. But neither one was willing to tip the tenuous balance between them.

Despite Matt's flirting, he made no moves to push their relationship into anything deeper. He liked to touch. It was part of his nature, and Julie tried not to let the casual hugs and embraces bother her, but it was difficult. The macho hero was turning out to be a nice guy, one she would like for a friend at the very least. If only he didn't play baseball.

But he did, and it was the one thing that continued to keep them apart. Julie couldn't bring herself to tell him the last little bit of truth about her father and their family. It was something that she tried to bury away, and despite his probing questions, she refused to open up. She was afraid that he would take her last defense and toss it aside, and then she would have nothing left to fight him with.

Matt stared up at Julie's apartment building, waiting for the door to open, preparing for the familiar tightness in his stomach that hit him every time he saw her face. The past two weeks had been a bittersweet mixture of heaven and hell. Julie was becoming more than just a challenge to him; she was getting under his skin, and he was beginning to feel distinctly unsettled.

He was committed to baseball and as much as he enjoyed relationships with women, he had always put them on the back burner, and if they weren't happy with the situation they left. It was all very cut-and-dried, neat and tidy. But with Julie, things were getting complicated. His goals were getting tangled up with long blond hair and deep brown eyes.

The door to her building opened and he caught his breath as she walked out into the late-afternoon sunshine. She was sex and innocence all mixed up in a lovely, conservative package that he was itching to unwrap. He swallowed back the knot in his throat as she joined him, and impulsively he reached out to hug her. She pulled away as she always did, but the soft look in her eyes was promise for the future. He smiled at her and opened the car door.

"I think you'll like Connie and Gary," he said conversationally. "They're wonderful people."

Julie forced a smile onto her face. The last thing she wanted to do was meet another baseball player, but

Matt's friendly invitation had left her little choice. "I'm sure they're very nice."

Matt smiled at her prim tone and then walked around the car and slid into his seat. He hoped he was doing the right thing asking Julie to meet his baseball friends. It was a gesture he rarely made to the women in his life. He preferred to keep them away from his close friends and family. But Julie needed to see that baseball was filled with good people.

"Where do they live?" Julie inquired, trying to still the feeling of tension that had enveloped her since Matt had told her of the invitation. It was one thing to spend time with Matt alone; it was another to have to socialize with other baseball players. What if they knew her father? What if they started asking questions? The old feeling of panic rose in her throat. She rolled down the window hastily and let the crisp air blow against her face.

"Are you all right?" Matt asked in concern.

"Fine. I just need some air. Is it too cold for you?"

"Not at all. You just look pale all of a sudden." He threw another sidelong glance her way.

"Overwork probably." She cleared her throat. "Where do your friends live?"

"Woodside," he answered, turning onto the freeway. "They have a beautiful house in the hills, very secluded and private. It's gorgeous. I hope it's still light when we get there so you can look at the grounds. It's a huge spread."

"But you said they don't have any children?"

"Not yet. They've been trying, but so far no luck. I know Connie is going crazy for a kid. Gary wants children, but I don't think he minds waiting."

"Sure. He's got his career," Julie said sharply, folding her arms in front of her.

Matt smiled and shook his head. "Connie has a career too. She's a writer. I'm sure one day we'll see an exposé on the baseball world from her, but right now she concentrates on childrens' books. She's a great storyteller."

Julie sighed at his easy explanation and offered him an apologetic glance. "I'm sorry, Matt. I'm a little tense about meeting another baseball player."

He reached out and took her hand, bringing it gently to his lips for a light kiss. "I know you're not happy about this evening, but I want you to meet my friends. I think you'll like them."

Julie threw him a glance and then looked out the window, her mind barely registering a beautiful setting sun in a royal blue sky. "Have you told them about me?"

"A little. I told them you were a wonderful, attractive woman who didn't think much of baseball."

Julie grinned at the description. "Did you really say I was attractive?"

"Actually I think I raved about you, but you don't want to hear the gory details."

"Actually I do."

"I didn't tell them about your father or your past, so don't feel pressured to talk about anything you don't want to talk about. This is just going to be a relaxing evening with a couple of friends. No stress."

"That sounds nice," she said, leaning back against her seat.

Chapter Six

Relaxing wasn't the word she would have used to describe Connie Hartman. Connie was a tiny woman with glorious red hair that fell down to her waist, an outgoing personality and a bright, lilting laugh that enveloped Julie like a warm hug. But she was also somewhat exhausting.

What she lacked in height, she made up for in energy. The minute they entered the house, Julie was swept away for a whirlwind tour of what she laughingly called the homestead, and they had no sooner settled in the living room, when Gary dragged Matt off to help light the barbecue. Julie was just catching her breath when the inevitable questions began.

"How long have you and Matt known each other?" Connie asked with a friendly grin, her hands busy pouring two glasses of wine.

Julie accepted the offering and smiled. The first question was easy enough. "A few weeks. I work for the

California Children's Foundation, and it was my duty to solicit Matt's help for our annual Celebrity Cook-off. He, in turn, roped in Gary and a few other Cougars."

"So, you're the one who wants to risk Gary's cooking."

"I'm sure it couldn't be worse than Matt's."

Connie grinned. "Nobody's cooking is worse than Matt's, but still he's a great guy, don't you think?"

"He's wonderful," Julie agreed hastily, taking a sip of wine.

"He's a fantastic baseball player, one of the best in the game right now and definite Hall of Fame material, don't you agree?"

Julie hesitated. "I've heard he's terrific."

There was surprise and curiosity in Connie's sparkling green eyes. "I guess you haven't seen him play."

"No, I haven't. We really just met." Julie said defensively and then shook her head in disgust. "I'm sure Matt told you that I'm not a baseball fan."

"He did mention it. I must admit I'm a bit surprised. But then again, perhaps you're just what Matt needs. He has more than enough adoring fans, but not one special woman," she added softly.

"There's nothing serious going on between us," Julie said bluntly, wondering why she felt the need to explain their relationship. It wasn't that Connie was particularly pushy. Maybe she was the one who needed a reminder.

"Whatever you say. It's none of my business what your relationship is with Matt, but I have to tell you that I consider him an honorary brother, and I worry about him just like he's part of the family. You're the first woman he's brought to meet us in a very long time. I admit I'm more than a little curious."

''We're friends at the moment.''

''Does that mean you're hoping for more?''

Julie laughed. ''No, it just means that we're not enemies. We have quite a few differences between us including our feelings about baseball.''

''Matt and Gary are obsessed with baseball,'' Connie agreed. ''I am, too. It's been a part of my life for so long, I can't imagine living without it.''

''You probably won't have to. Matt tells me that Gary is quite an athlete.''

''He is, but you never know what can happen. Gary was involved in an automobile accident about three years ago. His right leg was broken in three places. The doctors weren't sure he would walk without a limp, let alone play baseball. It was a terrible crisis point for both of us.'' She paused as she settled back in her seat.

A life without baseball sounded wonderful to Julie, but obviously not to Connie. The cheerful light had faded in her eyes as she remembered an obviously painful period in her life.

''I never thought I would feel so incredibly devastated,'' Connie continued, ''but I felt Gary's disappointment, his despair, so deeply that I wanted to run out there and somehow play for him.'' She smiled softly, her light tone belying the seriousness of her words. ''But thankfully I didn't have to. He made it back, mostly due to Matt's influence.''

Connie looked out the window to where Matt and Gary were leaning against the porch deck sharing a beer and stoking the coals. ''Matt was an inspiration to Gary. He never gave up on him. I don't think I can ever repay him for that.''

Julie followed her gaze, wondering why Matt had such influence over people—first Gary and now her. He was subtly and deliberately forcing her to examine her ideas, her thoughts, her feelings.

"Would you like another glass of wine?" Connie inquired, reaching for the bottle on the side table.

Julie shook her head. She needed to keep her wits about her. She was already feeling much too comfortable in the cozy living room, looking out the window, watching the final rays of sun descend behind a mountain of trees. It was hard to be bitter in this beautiful surrounding. It was hard to dislike anything including baseball. She turned her head away from the view and decided that as long as they were this far into the discussion, she might as well ask a few questions of her own.

"What would you have done if Gary hadn't been able to play baseball again?"

"I have no idea. I'm sure I could have adjusted, but I don't know about Gary. Baseball is his life, and believe me I know. We've been together sixteen years. We met when we were fourteen years old, and even then he was dreaming of a major league career. We've been through everything together, the minors, the farm systems of three baseball clubs and finally the majors. I've lived in more cities than I can count and seen more baseball stadiums than I ever dreamed possible."

Julie nodded, remembering her own gypsy existence. But she had been a child then; the memories were blurred by later problems. "Do you like being a baseball wife? Do you really like coming in second to the fans and the press and everything else?"

Connie's mouth dropped open, clearly startled by her words. "I don't come in second, Julie. Not now, not ever."

"Really?" She framed her words carefully, hesitant to say something offensive, but wanting to somehow work through the doubts that were plaguing her about Matt. "I've just heard that baseball can be very hard on wives. They're left alone a lot, and then there are the groupies always hovering around the guys, and the money and the glamour."

Connie started laughing. "It's true that sometimes these guys get stupid ideas about themselves and their own importance. That's where the wives come in. We just remind them of where they've been, and the next young star coming up behind them. As for the groupies, I don't worry anymore. I trust my husband."

"I'm sure you do. I guess you can't believe everything you hear." Or everything you see, she added silently to herself. Perhaps her father had been the exception and not the rule. She wanted to believe that was true more than anything in the world.

"Anyway, things are really coming together for us now," Connie remarked, rubbing a hand on her stomach as she snuck a glance out the window. "We're going to have a baby in the fall."

Julie's eyes widened in surprise at her unexpected announcement. "Congratulations. That's wonderful. Matt told me how much you like children."

"Yes. I'm very, very happy. We've been trying for a couple of years. Like I said, everything is really coming together for us. There's just one more thing that would make me happy."

"What's that?"

"For Matt to find someone special."

Julie shook her head. "Don't get your hopes up, Connie. Matt and I are worlds apart. He's a wonderful guy, but we just don't think along the same lines."

"I'm sorry to hear that. Matt's been so happy lately. When he talked about you, he got this look in his eye that just tugged at my heart. Do you know what I mean?"

Julie stared at her in disbelief. She knew that look exactly. It was the one she had described to Matt, the one she saw when he talked about his mother and his family. She smiled self-consciously but was saved from replying when the outside door burst open. Gary had obviously imparted the good news.

Matt reached for Connie and gave her a long, loving hug. "Congratulations. I can't believe it. This time next year there will be little Hartmans running around."

"Make that little Hartman, singular, please," Connie commanded, extricating herself with a laugh.

Matt smiled at Julie and then looked at his friends in wonderment. "I can't quite believe it. You two are going to be parents. That's more frightening than facing a ninety-mile-an-hour fastball."

"Tell me about it," Gary replied. "I don't even know how to prepare for it. I don't think you can practice for something like this."

Connie grinned and put an arm around her bewildered husband. "I think it just comes naturally."

"Yeah, I just wish the timing was a little better."

Connie nodded her head in agreement. "The baby is due in September which means a possible conflict with the end of the season and hopefully play-offs and the World Series," she explained for Julie's benefit. "We were hoping to avoid that problem, but when you've been trying as long as we have, you take whatever you can get."

Julie remained quiet as the others discussed the pending birth. She knew they were only joking about the conflict between baseball and baby; it was obvious that Gary and Connie were very excited about the prospect of becoming parents. But the mere fact that they had actually considered planning a baby around baseball season seemed somewhat cold-blooded. The old familiar bitterness crept around her like a well-worn blanket.

"Julie?" She realized Matt had repeated her name several times. Embarrassed, she apologized for her inattention. Connie sent her a shrewd look and then got to her feet.

"I'm going to get the rest of our dinner together, and Gary is going to put the chicken on," she announced with a long look at her husband. "And you two are going to sit here, have a drink and relax."

"I'd like to help," Julie protested.

"Later. You and Matt can do the dishes," Connie amended with a smile, pushing her husband into the kitchen.

"They're very nice," Julie remarked, looking over at Matt and wondering where his smile had gone. "Is something wrong?"

"I was going to ask you that same question. You became very quiet when Connie started talking about babies. Actually I think you became quiet when we started talking about baseball and babies."

Julie sighed and leaned back on the couch. "I don't want to argue. I can't help the way I feel. The reactions just happen without any control. It was a momentary thing. Don't blow it out of proportion."

"As long as you don't. We were kidding, you know. This baby is more important than baseball."

"I know it is."

"I don't want to feel like I have to watch everything I say."

Julie looked at him in surprise. "Please don't worry about it."

"Really? I don't want to offend you or hurt you, but sometimes the least little thing sets you off." He sat down next to her on the sofa and put his arm around her shoulders. "You're becoming very important to me."

His green eyes darkened with emotion as his words drew her closer to him than any embrace could. It was the look that got to her every time—so tender, almost loving. She had never met anyone like him.

"I feel the same way," she confessed. "But sometimes I don't want to."

His mouth spread into a slow smile and he placed a gentle whisper of a kiss on her forehead. "Don't fight it, sweetheart."

"Okay, I won't," she said with a gleam in her eyes. She placed a hand on each side of his face and after a long, deliberate pause, she leaned over and kissed him. Her lips fluttered softly against his, and then grew firmer as she deepened the kiss, sliding the tip of her tongue gently into his mouth.

Matt groaned and pulled her against him, prolonging the kiss until they were breathless. Shaken by the unexpected passion of what was meant to be a lighthearted kiss, they simply stared at each other for a long moment, and then Matt leaned back against the couch, closing his eyes.

Julie looked at him in confusion. "Matt?"

"Hmm?"

"Are you upset?"

"Yes," he replied, opening his eyes. "I'm upset that we can't finish this, that we have to exchange polite conversation for the next couple of hours when all I want to do is kiss you.''

Her heart stopped at the intensity in his voice. She knew exactly what he meant, but there was absolutely nothing she could say.

Abruptly, Matt stood up, extending a hand to her and pulling her to her feet. ''We need air, company and some good food.''

''I wish that was all we needed,'' Julie muttered to herself, following him out onto the deck.

The rest of the evening passed in a blur of pleasant conversation and amusing anecdotes. Matt and Gary had been friends since the minors, and they had hundreds of stories to tell about their experiences. Once in a while Matt offered her an apologetic glance and tried to steer the conversation away from baseball, but within minutes they would be right back where they started.

Julie felt a few twinges of pain now and then, but overall their experiences were amusing and light-hearted, and they opened her eyes to another side of baseball. They were both strong, confident men, but when they talked about their past, all the insecurities and fears of failure were revealed in their voices. She saw them not as they were today, proud and successful, but as they were in the past, young and desperate for a chance to prove themselves.

Their tales of the minor leagues of half-filled stadiums and booing fans were so real to her she could almost hear the jeers of the crowd, feel Matt's and Gary's insecurity when they stepped up to the plate. They talked about the long bus rides, the lousy motel rooms and the constant fear of not making it to the majors.

She had never thought of Matt as anything but a star, and he had never thought of himself as anything but a kid with a baseball bat and a dream.

The thought stuck with her throughout the evening and driving home later that night she was very quiet. Once again he had subtly twisted her emotions, introducing her to people who were impossible to dislike, forcing her to look at baseball from another perspective. Little by little he was peeling aside the defensive layers. A shiver racked through her body and she drew her sweater more closely around her.

"Here we are," Matt said, pulling up in front of her building. He turned off the engine and looked at her expectantly. "Can I come in?"

She knew he wanted to finish the kiss she had foolishly started at the Hartmans', but here in the dark, cosy interior of his car, she felt the danger more acutely than she had before. "It's late. I have to work tomorrow. Maybe we should just call it a night."

His look was long and hard. A mixture of emotions flitted through his eyes so quickly she felt utterly confused. "Sure, if that's what you want," he said finally. He opened the car door, got out and slammed it shut, leaving her sitting alone in the front seat. She hesitated and then joined him on the sidewalk.

"This evening was wonderful."

"I'm glad you had a good time," he said politely, as he walked her to the door. "I hope you weren't too bored talking baseball all evening."

Her lips curved into a wry smile. "Baseball does not bore me. In fact, that's probably the only emotion I don't feel."

"Right, you've made your feelings pretty clear. I guess I was hoping tonight might give you something to think about."

There was a hard, hurt edge to his voice that Julie couldn't ignore. "It did give me something to think about. That's why I want to be alone, to think. You and Gary really made me question the way I look at things. I'm sure that was the point of this evening, wasn't it?"

Matt's tension eased at the sincerity of her words. "I just want you to broaden your perspective. You saw your father through the eyes of a young girl. But you're a woman now. Perhaps there were a few things you missed back then."

"Before tonight, I would have said definitely not. But now I'm not so sure. I have to admit that I never thought of my father as anything but a baseball hero. But then I don't suppose we ever see our parents as they truly are, at least not when we're young." She sighed. "I don't know that I can ever forgive him, but perhaps I can stop blaming baseball for everything bad in my life."

Matt swept her into his arms as the last word left her mouth. He held her tightly against his chest, burying his face in the sweet fragrance of her hair. He had been afraid that she was pulling away, that the evening had backfired in his face. He hadn't realized how important it was to him until just this minute. "Thank God," he muttered into her ear.

Julie wrapped her arms around his waist, loving the feel of his arms around her, the deep emotion in his voice. Standing in the circle of his embrace, she wanted to believe that it would always be like this.

"This is it," Angela announced, as she and Julie took one last look at the Grand Ballroom of the Ambassador Hotel. "In one hour, this room will be filled with celebrities, press people and the cream of San Francisco high society." Her smile faded as panic set in. "I think I can wait."

"I know what you mean. It's going to be a madhouse," Julie remarked, looking for a discreet place to pin her foil-embossed name tag on her sapphire-blue silk dress.

Angela watched her with an amused smile. "Don't fight it, Julie. It has to go through the silk. Robert insists that the main staff wear name tags, just in case someone has a complaint or a problem."

"Or a compliment," Julie added optimistically, resolutely sticking the pin through her very new and expensive dress. "Tonight is going to be a tremendous success. I can feel it. Just look at this room. It's spectacular."

Her voice drifted off as they both took another sweeping look. Their hard work had paid off. The celebrity workstations were decorated in themes appropriate to each celebrity's forte, the bar was well stocked with both domestic and imported wines and the hotel staff was setting up a large buffet table in the middle of the room where guests of the cook-off would have an opportunity to sample the evening's entries.

"It looks good," Angela admitted. "The hotel outdid themselves. Now all we need are our celebrities and lots of generous patrons."

"They'll be here, and this year we'll be ready. We have place cards at every table and special badges for the press. I refuse to have a repeat of last year with Mrs. Hannington trying to squeeze twenty of her closest friends into the front table."

Angela rolled her eyes. "Good luck. Those people are going to be difficult, no matter what you do. By the way, how is your prize celebrity doing these days?"

"I assume you're referring to Matt."

"Yes, the overconfident, egotistical star you at one time professed to dislike."

"I hate it when people remember every little thing you say," Julie retorted, not taking offense at the obviously teasing comment. "He's fine. I admit he's much nicer than I first thought."

"He's done quite a bit for this event," Angela commented. "He helped record the radio spots, and even posed for a few pictures with some of the other celebrities. We can't ask for more than that. Although I have a feeling philanthropy is not his main motive."

Julie smiled to herself. "You've never questioned volunteer motives before."

"You're right. It doesn't really matter why they're here as long as they're here, and I don't want to pry. I just like to see you happy."

"I'm always happy. Sometimes I just don't show it."

"True. But there's an added sparkle in your eyes, and energy in your voice. Love."

"No," Julie said, refusing to even acknowledge the possibility. "Like, maybe, infatuation possibly, lust definitely, but not love."

Angela shook her head in mock despair. "Why not?"

Julie shrugged her shoulders, unable to confide in Angela the depth of her problem, the inevitable ties to her past. "I just don't think I could be in love with a baseball player. It doesn't seem important enough. It's a game."

"What difference does that make? So he's not a doctor or a missionary. He's a good man. He makes people happy just like you do. Baseball is entertainment, and it certainly has a place in this world.''

''Yes, I suppose so. I must admit that Matt adds a new dimension to my life. We've really gotten to know each other these last few weeks. It's been wonderful, even if it hasn't been real.''

''That's an odd thing to say. Do you think he's playing games with you?'' Her eyes filled with protective concern.

''No. But I think the time we've spent together is an exception to the rule. The last few weeks have been wonderful, but they've been make-believe. We've been hiding out in my apartment, wearing crazy disguises when we go out in public and in general, avoiding places with more than ten people in them. It has been fun, but it's just about over. For the next six months or so, Matt is going to be concentrating on baseball to the exclusion of everything and everyone else. I don't have any illusions about keeping a relationship going through the season.''

''Don't be silly. It may be hectic and busy, but you can find the time if you really want to,'' Angela replied persuasively. ''I don't think Matt is going to just let you walk away.''

Julie shook her head. ''I'm not really sure how Matt feels about me. I know he's attracted, interested, but I don't think he wants a long-term involvement. He's committed to baseball.''

''A lot of players get married.''

''And a lot of their marriages break up.'' Julie sighed. ''It's easy when we're alone together. I can pretend that baseball doesn't exist, that we're just two people sharing a meal, sharing our lives, but Matt leaves for Phoenix on Wednesday.''

"He'll be back. It's only for spring training."

"I know. But I wish he didn't have to go. I wish he was anything but a baseball player," she said wistfully.

"Then he wouldn't be Matt," Angela remarked. "He is what he is, Julie, just like you."

Julie sighed as her friend's words sank in. It was true. She couldn't separate Matt from baseball. She already knew how deeply he felt about his profession. It was a part of him. The need to play baseball was as important to him as eating and breathing. She was sure that love could never be equal in value. That's what saddened her the most. But she was trying to be optimistic, and somewhere deep down in her soul, she couldn't help hoping they could find a way to be together.

"Julie?" a voice called from the doorway.

Both women turned around in surprise, and then Julie smiled as Connie Hartman walked over. She was dressed in her finest evening wear—a stark black dress that made her hair seem redder, her smile brighter.

"Hello, Connie, how are you?"

"Fine, now that I've found you. Gary is coming straight from batting practice, and I wasn't sure I was in the right place."

"You are. This is Angela Moretti. Connie Hartman," Julie added, introducing the two women. "Connie is married to Gary Hartman, left fielder for the Cougars."

"Of course, I recognized your name," Angela said, extending her hand. "I'm looking forward to tasting his spaghetti sauce. The recipe looked very unusual."

Connie laughed. "It is definitely something you don't want to miss."

Angela looked at her watch and sighed. "It's almost time. I'm going to check with the banquet manager and make sure everything is on schedule."

Julie nodded. "Why don't you keep me company while I set up the front desk, Connie. I'm sure Gary will be here in a few minutes."

"I'd like that. You look absolutely gorgeous tonight, by the way. I can't wait to see Matt's face." Connie pulled up a chair, while Julie ducked embarrassedly behind the front desk and pulled out the place cards.

"I'm sure Matt will be too busy creating his deluxe hot dogs and chili to notice. I just hope he doesn't poison the judges."

Connie laughed. "He's a terrible cook. But he has so many other talents, it's probably justified. I hate to think anyone is perfect. Anyway, I'm sure the media will be so busy asking him baseball questions, he won't have time to do much more than stir the chili."

Julie frowned slightly. The image of Matt surrounded by the press and his fans bothered her. It was something that she had avoided thinking about during the past few weeks, and it had been easy to do so. She and Matt had spent time together but rarely in public. She wasn't sure she was ready for tonight.

"I just hope he finds time to plug the foundation. I'd hate to see the whole evening turn into a baseball press conference." Her words came out more sharply than she had intended, reflecting her insecurity, her fears.

Aside from one slightly arched eyebrow, Connie let the comment pass. "I wouldn't worry. Matt is very good at interviews. He won't disappoint you."

"I hope not." She wished she was only talking about the evening and not about the rest of her life. Taking out the place cards, she began to sort them into alphabetical order.

"Can I help?" Connie asked. "I might as well make myself useful."

"Sure. You can set these up alphabetically. That way we'll be able to find them quickly."

Connie nodded in pleasant agreement. "I'm glad I have a minute to talk to you, because I wanted to ask you about something."

"What's that?" Julie asked absently.

"Softball. Some of the wives and girlfriends play on a women's softball team in San Mateo. It's just one night a week for an hour, but it's really a lot of fun. We get so tired of just watching games all the time, that this lets us blow off some of our own steam, plus the guys get to do the watching and the baby-sitting for a change."

"Sounds like a good idea."

"I'm glad you think so, because we need you to play."

Julie's mouth dropped open, and she immediately started shaking her head.

"Don't say no. We have a great time, and it doesn't matter how well you play. It's a recreational league. No one is competitive."

Julie smiled in spite of herself. She could probably play better than most of the women, but she certainly had no intention of ever picking up a bat again. Just because she was opening herself up to Matt didn't mean that she was going to change her mind about baseball. That part of her life was over for good. "Thanks for thinking of me, but I really don't have time."

The hopefulness on Connie's face faded as her mouth puckered into a frown. "I'm not going to take no for an answer, mainly because we're desperate for players. Just think about it. The season doesn't start until next month. Perhaps your schedule will slow down a bit."

"I doubt it, but I'll let you know."

"You really don't like baseball, do you?"

"It's a long story, Connie."

"Okay, I won't interfere, especially since your big event is about to start, but someday we're going to have a long conversation...." Her voice trailed off at Julie's suddenly tense expression. "Is something wrong?"

"No, I just get nervous before big events."

"I'm sorry I brought up the softball. I didn't mean to upset you."

"You didn't. It's just this evening, and I suppose because Matt is going to be here, I feel everything even more intensely. I want this night to go well for everyone. I want it to be perfect."

"It will be. Don't worry," Connie advised, her fingers flying through the stack of place cards as they finished setting up the front desk.

Chapter Seven

Don't worry, Julie thought, as she walked slowly through the crowded ballroom. Two hours had passed since her conversation with Connie. The cook-off was in full swing, and she was still worried. Everything looked perfect. The crystal chandeliers in the ballroom glittered brightly, shimmering off the sequin-studded dresses and echoing off the continual flash of light from the cameras. But she still couldn't relax, and it had everything to do with Matt.

They had only had time for a brief hello before he was whisked away with the other celebrities to begin cooking. It was what she had expected; in fact, she had planned the schedule herself, but suddenly faced with his incredible popularity and unavailability, she felt irrationally upset.

Pushing her foolish emotions aside, she took her first break of the evening and strolled through the room, smiling politely at friends and volunteers. Her efficient eyes took in every little detail, and she stopped a few times to make sure that the celebrities had everything they needed and that the media were getting interviews and photo opportunities. She saved Matt's station for last—not that she had much choice—the area around him was packed with spectators.

Her official badge allowed her to slip through the crowd and after a moment she was able to get to the front of the gathering where she found Matt, dressed in an elegant black tuxedo that took her breath away. She just stood and stared at him as the other women were doing, wondering how one man could look so good. He had complained for days about having to wear a tuxedo. But here he was, looking like he'd been born into elegance.

He didn't see her standing there; he was too busy fielding questions from the press and smiling for the cameras. He was charming and confident and even a little bit cocky, but the crowd loved him.

Julie stiffened when a beautiful young socialite stepped forward and asked him to pose for a picture. The black-haired beauty was more than a little interested in Matt, lingering a few moments after the photo was taken to exchange small talk. Their conversation was too soft to be heard, but there was no denying the flirtatious quality of their exchange.

Standing behind the cordon of rope that separated Matt from the rest of the crowd, Julie felt as though she were invisible, and the feeling was very familiar. It could have been her father she was watching. But it wasn't, she tried to tell herself. Matt was not her father. He was warm and sensitive; he cared. But the little voice inside her was screaming a warning. Matt was a baseball player. He was a star. And tonight he was different; there was no question about it.

Silently she turned away and got back to work, refusing to acknowledge that Matt's public personality had disappointed her. She didn't know what she had expected him to do. He was an outgoing person. He was confident. But in front of the crowd, he had seemed bigger than life—a star. She didn't want a star; she wanted an ordinary man.

She was standing restlessly by one of the punch bowls when Matt finally found her. She had deliberately stayed away from him, trying to rid herself of a growing sense of unease and distrust. Despite their distance throughout the evening, her eyes had constantly strayed in his direction. He was so popular, it was frightening, and she felt more than a little inadequate. She didn't want to compete. She was afraid she would lose.

"Hi, sweetheart," he said lightly, flinging a casual arm around her shoulders and kissing her gently on the cheek.

"Something wrong?" he asked when she pulled away.

"Nothing. I'm still a little tense."

"Why? The cook-off was fantastic, raised a fortune and no one got sick from eating my chili."

She tried to smile, but it was forced, and his eyes narrowed speculatively.

"Something is wrong. What happened?"

"Nothing. I just can't rest until everything is over."

"Everything is over. The judging is complete, the waiters are clearing the tables and it's time for you to relax. Angela is dancing, and you and I are dancing," he added pointedly, taking her hand under his arm.

"No," she protested, pulling back. "I really should keep an eye on things, but you go ahead. I'm sure there are dozens of women here who would like to dance with you." Julie hugged her arms around her waist and stared fixedly at the crowd. "I'm sorry. I'm just not used to dating someone who's everybody's pinup poster boy."

"Come on, Julie, give me a break. I want to dance with you, all right?"

She wanted to refuse, but he was difficult to resist. He pulled her into the middle of the dance floor where the lights were low and there was intimacy, despite the crowd.

She held herself stiffly for a few minutes, but the song of love tugged at her heart, and Matt's arms tightened around her waist as he pulled her closer into his embrace. Her head came just under the tuck of his chin, and she closed her eyes against his chest, as the heat built within her.

Her hand slid into the base of curls at his neck, caressing the warmth of his skin, as his own hands made a seductive travel up and down the back of her silky dress, his fingers lingering at the expanse of skin revealed by her plunging back neckline.

As the beat of the music swept seductively through her body, he pulled her against him, dancing so closely that their legs were intertwined. It was the closest they had ever been. The quiet evenings in her apartment had often been fraught with tension, but never had she felt such an emotional pull to a man. She took a quick look at him and then dropped her gaze. She was afraid of what he would see, what he would think. Hopelessly she closed her eyes, and rested her head against his broad shoulder, wishing they were alone, and thanking God that they weren't.

The music finally ended, bringing their momentary peace to an abrupt halt. Reality intruded as a beautiful young woman put a hand on Matt's shoulder.

"May I cut in?" she asked smoothly, not at all put off by Matt's frown.

"I don't think—"

Julie interrupted his protest. "I have to get back to work."

The woman stepped between them with satisfaction, and the music began again. Julie watched them from the sidelines, refusing to acknowledge Matt's grim looks. She had forced him into the dance. Why did it hurt so much to see another woman in his arms?

"Are you okay?" Angela asked worriedly, coming up behind her.

"Sure. Fine. Tonight has been wonderful. No problems, lots of donations. It's been perfect."

"Are you done?" Angela asked when she finally ran out of steam.

"Finished, completely finished."

Angela nodded wisely. "It's hard to be in love."

"I'm not in love."

"Sure. Right. See you later."

"I'm not in love," Julie repeated, ignoring a stranger's look of surprise. Turning away in disgust, she finished her duties.

"When can you leave?" Matt asked quietly, from behind her just as she finished packing up the extra brochures in the reception area.

"Not until it's over and everyone has gone home."

"We need to talk. I'll wait for you."

Julie stepped out from under his possessive arm. "You don't have to wait for me. It will be very late before I'm through. I'll just go home and go to bed. I'm exhausted."

"I'm sure you are. But I don't want you driving home all alone. I'll wait."

"I drive home alone all the time. I can handle it."

"You don't have to handle it. I'll wait."

She opened her mouth to protest and then closed it. What was the point? She had to face him sooner or later. "All right. I'll see you in a while. I want to check on everything."

"I'll wait for you in the front, Julie. Take your time. I'm not going anywhere without you."

She smiled at the irony of his words. He wasn't going anywhere tonight, but in three days that would change. His life would be an endless circle of baseball games and road trips. He would be going a lot of places without her.

The bright lights of Matt's car stayed right behind her during her trip across town. It was comforting to know he was there, but she also felt tense about how to handle their situation. When she was away from him, every cold rational argument about their relationship played through her mind. But when they were together, she found herself wavering, fighting off an emotional desire to be with him, if only for a little while. The ride to her apartment passed swiftly, and she was no closer to a decision than she had been when she left. She pulled into the garage so that Matt could get his car off the street, and then she waited for him to join her.

He followed her up the stairs silently, so different from his usual teasing self, that her worry deepened.

With a sigh, she unlocked the door and turned the lights on. "Do you want a drink or something? I can make some coffee."

"No, I want to talk."

"What about?"

"You. Us. Whatever you feel we need to talk about."

"Okay. Let's talk about what happened tonight," she said quietly as they faced each other across the room.

"What happened?"

"Seeing you tonight in all your glory was like watching my father all over again. I was on the sidelines, and you were the star, facing your proud, adoring public."

Matt's eyes widened in surprise and then frustration at the inevitable bitterness in her voice. "Tonight's event was set up that way. In fact, you set it up that way. The people who came tonight wanted to see Matt Kingsley, superstar baseball player. They wanted me to act a certain way, and in return they dumped money into the foundation. Isn't that why I was asked to participate? I thought I was doing what you wanted."

She hesitated. "I suppose from a professional standpoint I couldn't have any complaints. But personally speaking, your attitude tonight was all too familiar."

"What did I do that was so terrible?"

"I can't pinpoint it exactly. It wasn't one thing. It was your overall attitude. You were so confident and you acted like you were putting on a show."

"I was," he yelled impatiently, running a hand through his already tousled hair. "Do you know how hard it is to stand in front of that many people and have to answer their questions regardless of how personal or provocative they might be? Do you have any idea how difficult it is to be famous? Do you?" He was so furious, he felt like shaking her. "Everyone wants a piece of me. Do this, do that, smile for the cameras, dance with my wife, kiss my baby. Lord, I'm sick of it. And you're no different, Julie. You used me, too.''

"How can you say that? I would never use you."

"Sure you would. You used me tonight just by asking me to participate. Your motives might have been good, but it's still the same. You wanted Matt Kingsley, celebrity, to appear at your cook-off so that you could raise more money. Your foundation wanted the star, not the man. And that's what I gave you. I'm sorry if you're disappointed.''

She stared at him in shock, wondering how their conversation had gotten so convoluted. She was suddenly confused; he was twisting everything around.

"You don't understand."

"I think I do. I'll let you in on a little secret, Julie. Before I met you I always wondered if a woman was with me because of who I was or how much money I made. I was never really sure if they just wanted to date a star baseball player or if they wanted to see me. But with you I never had to worry about that. I thought our feelings were honest and out in the open. I thought you understood that I'm a man first and a baseball player second.''

"It just didn't look that way tonight,'' she said helplessly.

He stared at her for a long moment and then turned away. He didn't say another word, just walked out of the room, slamming the door with a finality that frightened her more than his words.

Julie awoke the next morning with a pounding headache and a fierce desire to break something in half. It wasn't like her to be emotional—not anymore. She had buried that side of her personality the day her father walked out. But Matt had brought everything back to the surface, the torn-up emotions, the feelings of rejection and of desire. She wanted to be loved, just like everyone else. Yet once again she had chosen the wrong man to love, someone who couldn't possibly give her what she needed.

It was over. There would be no more lingering talks over pizza and wine, no more cooking lessons, no more Matt and definitely no more baseball. The thought should have made her happy, but it didn't.

She spent the rest of the weekend cleaning her apartment and trying to bury the memories, but the loneliness of her home only served to remind her of how alone she was. Her mother had someone, her father probably had dozens of someones and she had nobody but herself and her job. It was the only thing left in her life that brought her any kind of happiness.

With that thought in mind she awakened on Monday, ready to face the world again. She welcomed the daily ritual with open arms, eager to get back into the safe, comfortable routine she had been happy with until Matt entered her life. She looked forward to the long hours of follow-up calls on cook-off donations and the chance to devote herself to her work.

Her good mood lasted exactly thirty minutes which was how long it took to get from her apartment to the office. When she got out of her car, she saw Matt waiting outside the door to her building. He was perched on the side wall looking out at the wharf with a decidedly grim expression that was quite at odds with the scenic view of colorful sailboats and choppy, blue water. For a moment she was tempted to run in the other direction, but then he turned and saw her.

"Good morning," she said quietly, pausing in front of him.

"Hi." His voice was low and intense, matching the somberness of his expression.

"Were you waiting for me?"

"Yes. I wanted to talk to you before I leave."

She bit down on her lip. "Where are you going?"

"I'm leaving for Phoenix today instead of Wednesday. There doesn't seem much point in hanging around." He waited for her to deny his statement, but she was silent. "That's what I thought."

He slid off the wall and turned to leave, and instinctively she caught his arm. "I wish things could be different."

Matt stared down at her misty brown eyes and felt a touch of guilt. She looked pale and tired and very vulnerable. He had never wanted to hurt her. With his usual confidence he had just jumped in, thinking he could beat the bitterness buried within her, break down those walls and show her that he was different.

"There's nothing I can say, is there?" he asked, feeling another wave of frustration rush through him.

"No. But there's something I want to say." She paused for a long moment, picking her words carefully. "I do care about you. You're a wonderful man. It's just everything that comes with you. I have too many memories, too many disappointments. I don't think I'm ever going to be able to trust in you or in us. I don't like the way I've been acting, judging you, always believing the worst, but I can't seem to control it. I'm sorry. It just hurts too much."

"Yeah, it does hurt." He stepped closer to her and tilted her chin up with his hand so that she was forced to look into his eyes. "I want you to think about me,

Julie. I want you to think about us and everything that we could have together. I want you to think about this." He lowered his head and kissed her—a long, passionate kiss that was filled with frustration and longing and incredible desire. And then he was gone, leaving her alone with the sunshine, the sounds of springtime and a deep pain in her heart.

Four weeks had passed since Matt had left for Phoenix, and each one had felt like a million years, Julie thought as she crossed another item off her To Do list. Work had kept her busy, but even the hectic chaos of the upcoming walkathon had done little to push Matt out of her mind or out of her heart. She found herself thinking of him at odd times and when she tried to sleep at night, her dreams were filled with his image.

Now that the Cougars were heading back to San Francisco after a successful spring training, the newspapers and television broadcasts were filled with baseball, and Matt Kingsley was always on the top of the list. Despite her efforts to avoid hearing about him, she would inadvertently catch sight of his face during a news interview or see a photo in the newspaper. And the thing that bothered her the most was his familiar teasing smile. He didn't look sad at all—not like the man who had walked away from her four weeks ago. Baseball had obviously worked its magic.

Despite her efforts to be cheerful and happy, her smile was always a little forced, her walk a little less jaunty, and of course, their resident psychologist, Angela, couldn't resist making a comment.

"Food for the weary, the hungry, and the brokenhearted," Angela announced, breaking into her thoughts and her office with a cheerful grin. She waved a delicious-smelling brown bag in front of Julie. "Lunchtime."

"I'm not hungry."

"Of course you're not hungry. You never are. But you have to eat. I refuse to watch you get any thinner while I go the other way." Angela began clearing off Julie's desk and opening the containers.

"What did you get?" Julie asked, the rumble in her stomach reminding her that her last meal had been hours ago.

"Chicken chow mein, sweet and sour pork, rice and of course, fortune cookies. I'm hoping mine will predict a tall, dark, handsome stranger. I'm hoping yours will predict a certain brown-haired, green-eyed superstar."

"Thanks but no thanks. I'm just fine on my own."

Angela snorted in disgust. "Hardly. You've been moping for days."

"I've been working down at the halfway house. It always makes me feel a little down. The people there have so many problems, it's sad."

"That's true," Angela said seriously. "I thought being there might have made you realize how good you have it."

"You think I'm being selfish."

"No. Foolish. You're in love with Matt Kingsley. Why don't you do something about it?"

"Because I don't want to be in love with him."

"Why not?"

Julie shook her head, her long hair hiding the pain in her eyes. "It's too long a story to explain."

"Someday you're just going to have to trust someone," Angela said wisely. "I've watched you turn down just about every man that asks you out."

"That's not true."

"Or you go out on a few dates and then find something terribly wrong with the guy and before you know it you're back to square one."

"There just aren't that many good men out there," Julie argued, unwilling to admit there was a thread of truth in Angela's comments.

"Then for goodness' sake, don't let Matt Kingsley slip through your fingers. I saw the two of you together. I saw how good things were."

"Appearances can be deceiving."

"I know that, but I don't think I'm wrong about him. So, tell me, what are you going to do?"

"I don't know. I should probably move to another city or another country, then I wouldn't have to hear that Kingsley is king every time I turn around."

"Don't kid yourself. The man has been doing ads in Japan. He's an international star."

"If that was supposed to make me feel better..."

"It wasn't. You know that I believe in facing your fears."

"How could I forget?"

"So I have an idea," Angela continued, ignoring her interruption. She reached into her pocket and drew out two tickets. "Go with me to opening day."

Julie looked at her in amazement. "Opening day to what?"

"The Cougars, of course."

"You've got to be kidding. I have no desire to go to a baseball game. If you were talking symphony or ballet, maybe, but not baseball."

"We're not going to watch the game, we're going to see Matt." She shook her head warningly as Julie started to refuse. "I'm not going to take no for an answer."

"Angela, I am not going to sit there and watch thousands of women drool over Matt's body in baseball pants. So forget it."

"Ah hah! So you have thought about Matt's body in baseball pants. Now I know you're ready to go."

"I'm not going."

"Face your fears."

Julie groaned. "Oh, please. Disliking baseball is hardly a fear. Besides I just don't want to see Matt."

"Because you're afraid."

"No, I'm not."

"Then prove it. Go to the game with me. I got these tickets from the president of our board. He says the seats are terrific, and this is a perfect opportunity for you to see Matt without any pressure. You'll just be one of thousands of drooling women as you call them, although there might be a few who are actually interested in the game itself. Seriously, I think that seeing him will help you finalize things in your own mind. You can definitely decide that you don't want him, that you're not in love. On the other hand . . ."

"There is no other hand." Julie paused for a long moment, wavering slightly.

"Then what do you have to lose?"

Julie threw up her hands in defeat. "All right. I give up, I'll go. But I warn you, I am not going to have a good time."

Chapter Eight

Opening day was blessed with brilliant sunshine, a warm breeze and the sparkling laughter of thousands of fans eager to embrace the beginning of a new baseball season. Sitting in a reserved box behind first base, Julie was finding it difficult to remember why she hated baseball. Despite her intentions to sulk, the holiday mood was slowly seeping into her.

She was all alone for a moment, having sent Angela off for some hot dogs and drinks, and she had a chance to think, something she had been putting off doing for a long time. Her first glimpse of Matt in his baseball uniform had sent her heart racing. Even in the distance she could make out his broad shoulders, the curly hair creeping out from under his cap, the long, lean legs moving gracefully as he warmed up. Of course, she wasn't the only one watching. He wasn't just a baseball player, he was a sex symbol, and the crowd loved him.

Tearing her eyes away from him, she forced herself to look around the stadium, to remember the old, familiar feelings of pain and bitterness, but they were difficult to grasp. Watching the crowd, hearing the laughter, smelling the hot dogs, seeing the smile on a wide-eyed child made her feel like she had awakened from a deep sleep. Baseball was a game of joy and of love. It brought families and friends together to share a day in the sun, to laugh together, to live life. How could she have forgotten that?

"Julie? Are you all right?" Angela asked with some concern, noting the dazed expression on Julie's face as she sat down. She set the carton of hot dogs and drinks on the empty seat next to them and turned to face her friend.

"Fine."

"Did I miss something, or did you just change from a depressed woman into a happy-go-lucky lady?"

"It just happened. It's this place," she said, sweeping her hand out in front of her. "I forgot how much fun people have here."

"If you think this is good, wait till the game starts."

"I'm starving," Julie added, accepting a hot dog from Angela and laughing when the mustard squirted out in all directions as she took a bite.

"I'm glad you're having a good time. I thought seeing Matt again might wake you up, although I must admit I didn't expect it to happen quite so soon."

"It's not Matt, at least not totally. It's everything that I had associated with baseball. I had some bad memories. Someday I'll tell you all about it. But right now I just want to sit back and enjoy myself."

"Good, and you can tell me what's going on. I don't know a thing about this game, but I have a feeling you know more than just a little."

Julie smiled and chewed thoughtfully on her hot dog as the Cougars took the field.

Nine innings didn't seem enough, and she was almost sorry when the Cougars won in the bottom of the ninth. She was reluctant to let go of the happy feeling that had enveloped her during the game. But there were some decisions to make and a lot of talking to be done. She hoped she hadn't left things too late.

They waited patiently for the crowd to disperse after the game, each wondering what the next move would be. When Julie finally stood up decisively, Angela followed without saying a word. She didn't question their descent to the mezzanine level or their sudden abrupt stop in front of the clubhouse door. She just waited patiently.

Julie groaned at the familiar sight of waiting women. She should have known better. The ropes and guards were set up for one reason—to protect the guys from the girls—and Julie was not going to be an exception. In some ways it was a laughable thought, protecting big, strong men from a group of women, but then again, she knew just how obsessive the fans could get. She turned to Angela with a gleam in her eye.

"Would you mind if—"

"If you waited for Matt? No. I wouldn't mind. But are you sure you're going to be able to see him?"

"He has to come out eventually. But I'm not planning on waiting here. I have another idea. Are you sure you don't mind? I haven't ditched a girlfriend for a boy since I was fifteen. I feel kind of silly."

"The last time I let someone ditch me for a boy was when I was fifteen. But don't worry, as all good girl-friends do, I intend to go on by myself. I certainly wouldn't want to stand in the way of love."

"Not love."

"Good luck. Call me if you find yourself stranded. I'm going to go back to the office and work off some of the guilt I have for spending a weekday at the ball-park."

"Don't remind me. I've been trying not to think of all the work waiting for me. Thanks for being so understanding and for making me come today. I owe you one."

"You certainly do. Why don't you find out if any of those other players are available? I'm beginning to like a man in a uniform—very sexy."

Julie grinned as Angela walked away. Now that she was alone, she hesitated, unsure what course to follow. Finally, she walked out into the parking lot. There was a reserved area for players, but she didn't see the red Ferrari. Walking a little farther into the preferred parking area, she finally spotted it parked against the bush-lined fence and nearly hidden from view. She walked over to Matt's car and leaned casually against the hood, preparing herself for a long wait.

As the minutes passed, the parking lot slowly emptied leaving Julie sitting alone on top of Matt's car. A few of the other players had walked by, giving her a strange look as they got into their cars and drove away. They probably thought she was a groupie. She wished she had seen Connie or Gary. She knew they could have gotten her into the inner sanctum, but in a way she was relieved to be on her own. She wasn't sure how Matt felt anymore, or if she had read too much into a few weeks of casual dating.

The sun had just dipped behind the horizon when Matt walked through the now-silent parking lot. His shoulders were slumped, his face tense as he came toward the car, and she wondered if she had chosen the wrong time. But it was too late. He had seen her, and the startled expression in his eyes did little to help her gauge his feelings.

"Hello," she said, as he walked over to her.

"Julie. What are you doing here?" His voice was carefully neutral.

She slid off the car as he dropped his athletic bag on the ground and stared at her. There were shadows under his eyes and his mustache trailed into the beginnings of a beard along his cheekbones. He looked more serious than she had ever seen him—certainly not like an athlete celebrating his first win of the season.

"I had to see you," she said finally.

"Why?"

"You're not going to make this easy for me, are you?"

"Should I? The last time we spoke you implied you never wanted to see me again. Now, here you are."

"I changed my mind."

He crossed his arms in front of him aggressively. "Good for you. If you'll excuse me, I have to go. I'm very tired. It was a long game."

"I know. I saw it. You were wonderful, especially your clutch hit in the ninth."

"You saw the game?" he asked incredulously, the grimness in his face lightening with surprise. "I can't believe you saw the game."

"I did. Every minute. I didn't even get up for popcorn."

"Why? Do you need me to do another fund-raiser perhaps, or was the foundation trying to solicit donors at today's game?" He ran a hand through his hair in angry frustration. "Dammit, Julie, what happened?"

"I'm trying to tell you," she burst out. "Everything happened. You and Angela, and the damned sports page. Everywhere I turned I saw your name, I heard your voice. I wanted to forget about you. I wanted to forget about baseball, and God knows I tried, but I couldn't do it. I've been so unhappy and confused since you left, I don't know what I'm doing half the time. And then Angela came into my office with a ticket to today's game, and insisted that I come. She was right. I did need to come here today."

She paused, searching for the right words. "I had forgotten how much I used to like baseball, how much fun it is. Looking around at the park today, I realized that I've shut myself off from a game that is pretty enjoyable."

Matt stared at her in shock, his feelings of happiness mixed with uncertainty. He had spent four weeks telling himself that there was no room for someone like Julie in his life. He needed to concentrate on baseball, not get tangled up in a love affair filled with messy complications. It wouldn't be fair to either of them. But as his eyes roamed restlessly over her beautiful face, he knew he wasn't going to be able to walk away. Not yet.

"Say something, Matt," she urged.

"I don't know what to say."

"Then could you just hug me?" she whispered.

The familiar lazy grin spread over his face, and he felt happier than he had in weeks. He reached out and pulled her into his arms, squeezing her so tightly she could barely breathe. "I've missed you," he muttered, burying his face in her hair.

"I missed you, too," she said softly, turning her face up to kiss him.

Their lips touched hungrily, passionately, and they laughed breathlessly with the sheer joy of being together. Matt planted tiny kisses all over her face, his arms locking around her so that she couldn't move. And she didn't want to move. She wanted to bury herself in his arms, to hold on to him so that he could never leave her again.

"Perhaps we should take this somewhere more private," Matt suggested, as a group of teenagers whistled on their way through the parking lot.

Julie flushed with embarrassment. "We're making a scene."

"Not yet, but we will be if we stay here much longer. Then again, I've never made love on the hood of my Ferrari."

"Matt!"

"I'm kidding, just kidding. Seriously, do you have your car or are you coming with me?"

"Coming with you."

"Good." He reached around her to unlock the door, stealing a kiss behind her ear as he did so. "Hop in."

He closed the door behind her, and walked around to his side, tossing his athletic bag in the trunk before he took a seat. "Where do you want to go?"

She hesitated. "Somewhere private where we won't have to fight off the autograph hunters."

Matt looked at her for a long moment and then out at the empty parking lot, his mind obviously wrestling with a decision. Finally, he turned the key in the ignition. "We'll go to my house."

Within minutes they were on the freeway heading down the peninsula toward Foster City. They didn't talk much on the way. The evening traffic was rather heavy, and Matt had to devote all his concentration to his driving. Julie was grateful for the respite. She had gone through so many emotions in one afternoon that she felt like she needed to catch her breath. Finally, Matt pulled off at the Foster City exit and a few minutes later turned into a driveway in front of a very modern two-story home on a quiet, residential street.

Julie looked at the structure thoughtfully as Matt let her into the house. It was a picture of suburban living and about as far removed from the life of a flashy superstar as anything she had ever seen. The interior of the house was homey, and everywhere she looked there were plants.

"You have a green thumb," she remarked.

Matt made a face. "My mother has a green thumb. She sends me a new plant every month, and then I have to kill myself trying to keep them alive. I try to tell her that I don't have time for plants especially during baseball season, but she thinks it's the next best thing to a wife or a pet." His voice broke off abruptly. "Damn, that didn't come out right."

Julie walked over and put a finger against his lips. "You don't have to watch everything you say. I know what you mean, and personally I agree. I'm not much good with plants, either, and I do come home every night. But it doesn't seem to matter. They still wither and die as if I had left them to starve in a frozen wasteland."

Matt grinned. "I knew it. We're soul mates."

Julie walked down the hallway, curious to learn more about his bachelor life. At the back of the house was a large, comfortable family room with an attached redwood deck that provided a scenic view of the bay. The house was so normal, so ordinary, it was astounding.

"I don't get it. This house looks like something I would live in. Not a place for someone like you. Of course, I would have to make about twice as much as I do now," she amended.

"I told you I'm not any different than you are."

"Yes you are. You're a very attractive, eligible bachelor, not to mentic extremely rich."

"I like the first part."

"Is this house really you?"

"It is. Every last inch. There are no circular beds, black satin sheets, nothing particularly decadent, although I would be happy to improvise."

"I like it."

Matt walked over to her and put his hands on her shoulders. "Good. Because I like you."

Her heart stopped at the intensity of each word, and she didn't know who moved first, but suddenly they were in each other's arms, showing each other all the things they had not been able to put into words. The desire between them flared like a match to dry tinder. There was no slow buildup of passion; the fire blazed out of control with one long kiss.

Julie let her hands wander freely down his back and around his waist. She pushed her body provocatively against his, enjoying the long touch between them, the press of her breasts against his muscular chest, and the feel of his long lean legs intermingling with hers.

Matt grasped her hands and brought them up to his chest holding her against him while he stared down into her large, luminous eyes.

The question burned between them, and for just a second she hesitated. So much had happened in the past few hours, so many changes, realizations. Making love to Matt wasn't something she wanted to rush into, but then again she didn't think she could wait. She had never wanted anyone as much as she wanted him.

"Yes," she murmured, the words escaping without further thought. The flash of desire in his eyes made any resistance seem futile. It was going to happen between them as surely as the sun would rise. They were meant to be together. She raised her lips for his kiss, but Matt hesitated. She stared at him in surprise. Had she read the question wrong?

Matt shook his head. "No." He shook his head again. "No, I don't think so. I can't believe I'm saying that, but I am."

"Why?" she asked in confusion.

"Because you're not ready. Maybe because I'm not ready. Hell, I don't know. It's too fast. Yesterday I thought I would never see you again. Today, you show up at the ballpark, the answer to my prayers." His arms dropped from around her shoulders and he walked over to the window, taking a moment to think before he turned back around to face her. "I want you, Julie, but I want it to be perfect. No doubts, no reservations, no uncertainties. What do you think?"

She nodded her head slowly. "I think you're probably right." She smiled. "You're very sensitive."

"For a jock, right?"

His teasing tone broke the tension.

"Yeah, for a jock."

"Do you want a drink or something? Although I'm afraid beer is the only choice," he added, walking over to the refrigerator.

"A beer sounds great. It's in keeping with the spirit of today." She walked over to the window, taking a moment to catch her breath.

"Bottle or glass?" he asked.

"Bottle," she said, taking the beer from his hand.

"What did you think of the game? If you don't mind talking a little baseball," he asked with a smile.

"I thought Dale Howard should have called for a squeeze play in the bottom of the fourth. Mickey Jorgensen should have taken the second baseman out on his slide, thereby allowing Greg Hunt to be safe at first. And I think Stan Dolley should have thrown a slider at three and two against Larry Rickets."

Matt looked at her in astonishment. "Damn if I don't agree with you on everything but the slider. Fastball is the way to go on Rickets. He likes sliders."

"Yeah, well he likes curve balls better. He took that pitch to the fence. It was only Gary's fantastic barehanded catch in left that saved the day. Of course, I thought you were spectacular, making double plays look like child's play."

"Damn right," he teased. "I even hit a home run for you, although at the time I thought you would probably never even hear of it. You really do know baseball, don't you?"

"I used to be better, but I've lost a little insight in my absence from the game. And I don't know the players as well—their strengths, their weaknesses."

"Tell me something, Julie. Would you go out there again? Would you watch me play? Could you?"

"Yes. I think so." She paused for a long moment. "I have to admit that there are still things that bother me, and memories that hit me from every direction when I step into the ballpark. And, there is one more thing that I haven't told you."

"Another secret?"

"Actually I think it's just an extension of the first one. I never told you why my parents broke up, and I think it's time you knew the whole truth."

"Go on."

"It was after a play-off game. My father had just been named most valuable player, and my mother and I were surrounded by press wanting to know our reactions. We were so proud of him that night. Then a woman came up and interrupted the impromptu press conference. She had a girl with her, about six years old. She was a pretty little thing with dark blond hair." Julie's voice softened and then hardened again. "Her name was Michaela. She was my father's illegitimate daughter."

Matt stared at her, but he didn't say anything, just motioned for her to go on.

"He and this woman had been carrying on a long-term affair for at least six years. The woman lived in New York. I guess she was his East Coast love. Apparently, she got tired of waiting for a divorce, so she decided to take things into her own hands. I don't think I'll ever forget her face or the bewildered look on the little girl, my half sister."

"What did your father say?"

"I don't know. My mother and I walked out of the stadium, heads held as proudly as possible. My father and mother had a very loud argument later that night.

In the morning he was gone, and we were alone—again."

"It must have been a terrible shock."

"It was, not just because of the woman. I think my mother had known all along that there were other women, but she thought they were one-night stands, nothing permanent, nothing like what she had with my father. We were his family. That's what kept us going through all the absences. But when we found out that there was another family, another woman, another little girl, it made our relationship seem pointless." She shook back the tears. "The little girl said something that night, too. She told me that she was going to be a ballplayer like her dad—like my dad. I felt like I had been hit in the face. It was the one thing we shared—my ability to play ball. I was good. He was proud of me. But even that was shattered. Anyway, that's the last time I was in a baseball stadium until the day I came to find you. I guess baseball became the symbol for everything that went wrong."

"I'm sorry."

"But you don't seem surprised."

"I remember the story," he admitted.

Her jaw tightened. "I guess it was public knowledge, wasn't it? Why didn't you say something before?"

"I wasn't sure of all the facts, and I figured you would tell me when you were ready. I'm glad you did."

She turned around, feeling suddenly foolish and awkward. "I don't know why I kept thinking of it as a secret. I'm sure everyone in baseball knew about it. But my mother never let me read the papers or even listen to the radio after that night. She was trying to protect me, but it was too late."

"You must have had a rough time. I know that it's probably impossible for me to understand what you went through, but I do think it's a good sign that you were able to come to the ballpark today and even have a good time."

"Going back to the ballpark today was like going home for me. Everything was similar and yet different. I guess nothing is quite the same as you remember it."

"Maybe in your case that's a good thing."

She smiled. "You're probably right. Anyway, I think today I got rid of the last of the ghosts."

"At least the baseball ones," he said quietly, giving her a serious look. "But there's still your father to deal with."

"My father is not important anymore."

"Of course he is. You just don't want to admit it. But he colors your thinking, the way you react to men, to the idea of love, romance, commitment."

"Commitment," she echoed in disbelief. "You don't exactly have a history of commitment, either."

"We're not talking about me, we're talking about you."

"It goes both ways. I may have a few hang-ups, but I'm sure you do, too."

"Me? No way." With a grin, he got to his feet and pulled her into a standing position. "Let's get out of here, just spend some time together. Let's go to dinner. You can pick the restaurant—anything but pizza."

"Why not pizza? I thought it was your favorite food."

"It is. But I never eat it the night before a game."

She arched one eyebrow inquiringly. "Why?"

"Superstition. The last time I ate pizza before a game I went into a batting slump."

"That's ridiculous. Pizza doesn't have anything to do with your hitting." She paused, searching his face for any sign of humor or teasing, but he appeared to be completely serious. "What other little rituals are you hiding from me?"

His mouth crinkled into a smile. "Nothing particularly dangerous. Every athlete I know is superstitious. With me it's pizza and of course my sweatband." He reached over to the table and picked up a red-and-black wristband. "I have to wear this on my right wrist. It's my power."

"You're crazy. What happens if you lose your wristband? Do you lose your power?"

"I don't ever want to find out," he said seriously. "That's why I have half a dozen."

"So it's not just one particular band."

"No, but it has to look exactly like this one. I hit my first home run wearing this wristband."

Julie bit back a smile. "I don't suppose you've ever struck out wearing it."

"Sure I have, but that doesn't diminish its importance. It all has to do with feeling good when you step up to the plate. If something is off, like you change the part in your hair or you shave your mustache, you find yourself thinking about those things instead of the pitch. If I do the same thing every time, it betters the odds."

She held up a hand as his explanation began to escalate. "Okay, I believe you. We'll get Mexican food. You don't have any problems with that, do you?"

"No, in fact tacos are particularly lucky."

She rolled her eyes and walked toward the door. "You can tell me about it over dinner."

"And you can tell me why I struck out tonight," he added.

"You didn't," she replied with a pointed grin.

"Baseball, sweetheart. I'm talking baseball." He pushed her laughingly out the door.

Chapter Nine

" "Take me out to the ball game,' " Julie sang lightly as she exchanged her dress for a pair of blue jeans and a warm, black turtleneck sweater. Slipping her arms into her heavy down jacket, she gathered together her purse and a wool blanket to battle the unexpected bay breezes and with one last glance in the mirror, she headed out the door.

Tonight was a new beginning for her and for Matt. She was looking forward to going to the game, getting to know Matt's friends and learning more about the man she found so utterly appealing. She tried to act nonchalant, but it was a flimsy cover for her nervousness. The battle scars had faded, but the memories were not completely gone. She wondered what it would be like to go to a baseball game and not know any of the players personally. It would certainly be less exhausting emotionally, but probably not as much fun, she admitted as she drove to the stadium.

Matt had thoughtfully provided a parking pass and a ticket for her, so she was able to breeze right into the parking lot with little trouble. Her seat was in the players' section, and she was relieved to find herself sitting right next to Connie Hartman. It was a little daunting going into such a tight-knit group. Although the other women smiled at her, there was speculation in their eyes and wariness in their manners.

"Hi, Julie," Connie said cheerfully. "I'm glad you could make it. In fact, I'm thrilled." She leaned over with a confidential whisper. "I'm glad you two were able to patch things up."

"So am I. Looks like I made it just in time."

"We still have a few minutes so you can catch your breath. It must be difficult running from work to here. I have a feeling you're going to be exhausted by the end of the season."

"Yes, I'm a little worried about the schedule. I don't have a nine-to-five job. My hours are often long depending on the fund-raising campaign we're involved in, and I can't just check out to go to a ball game. Not that this isn't important, too." She prevaricated, trying to be sensitive to Connie's feelings.

But the other woman just laughed. "Don't worry about saying something to offend me. Baseball isn't a life-or-death matter. I'm very involved in it, dedicated, devoted, et cetera, but I also know that there are a lot of other things in this world that are far more serious. I think your job sounds wonderful and you certainly do a lot to help people."

"I hope so. Sometimes I get so caught up in the fund-raising end of the business that I forget why we do what we do. Every couple of weeks I try to visit some of the shelters and charities that we fund just to keep in touch with the needs of the people." Her voice trailed off as the audience swelled to their feet for the national anthem.

Julie sang softly under her breath as she stared at the flag blowing briskly in the wind. The singing of the national anthem always sent a chill down her spine. It was such a strange feeling to be part of a large crowd joined together for just one long moment in a mutual feeling of patriotism. She smiled as the singer hit the high note, drawing a round of applause and cheers from the crowd. Then it was time to play ball.

After the game, Connie led her down to the mezzanine level where there was a lounge reserved for friends and families of the players. She introduced her to some of the other wives, and Julie smiled and said hello and tried not to feel self-conscious. It wasn't surprising that they were curious about her. Matt was the star of the team. She just hoped she didn't let him down.

There were sandwiches and drinks set out on a side table, and she and Connie helped themselves while they waited for the men to shower and change.

"This is a wonderful buffet," Julie remarked.

"The Cougars are a very generous organization to the players and their families," Connie agreed, grabbing Julie's arm and pointing her in the other direction. "Get a look at that outfit."

Julie's eyes opened wide as a very tall brunette swaggered by, her curvaceous figure barely clothed in a skimpy red miniskirt and a tight red sweater. "Who is that?"

"Stephanie Holt, otherwise known as Miss February."

"I don't recall seeing her outside. She would have frozen to death in that outfit."

"She was probably sitting in one of the sky boxes. She has quite a few influential—friends, I guess you could say."

Julie stared in amazement as the other woman strolled up to the buffet table, her high-pitched voice drawing complete attention as she protested about the meager spread. She was followed by another woman who was dressed in a black miniskirt and leather jacket.

"Who are they with?"

Connie grinned. "Stephanie is with Buddy Jackson. He plays centerfield. The other girl—I think her name is Dana—she goes out with Greg Marlin or whoever else is available. She's a groupie."

"I know there are a lot of women who hang around the ballpark," Julie said slowly, her eyes still following the other two women. "But I didn't realize they came in and mingled with the wives and everyone else."

"Most of them don't. The hangers-on usually wait at the hotels when the guys are on the road or at some of the local hot spots." She paused. "I guess I should tell you since you'll probably hear it soon enough—Buddy's wife found Stephanie in their bed two weeks ago. She just filed for divorce."

Julie felt herself tense at the thought—another Jack Michaels. "How horrible," she said tightly.

"Buddy's a jerk. She's better off without him."

"Probably, but I'm sure it must hurt, especially to be embarrassed in front of your friends, or worse yet, pitied."

"Julie, are you okay? You look funny all of a sudden. You're not worried that Matt..."

"No, no of course not."

"Good, because he's not the type to fool around."

Julie looked at her skeptically. "I find that a little hard to believe. You don't have to paint such a perfect picture of him for me. I'm not going to hold his past against him."

"You're right. I'm acting like there's something to hide, and there isn't. He's a normal man, but I know he's never been particularly interested in one-night stands. Underneath those playboy looks lurks a very conservative, old-fashioned guy. He and Gary room together on the road when I don't go along," Connie added. "So they better not be fooling around."

"I'm sure they're not. It's just so hard not to worry. It's like taking a child to a toy store and saying 'Don't touch.' It must be difficult."

"But they're not children...." Connie reminded her, her voice trailing off as one of the players entered the room wearing a Cougar mask and brandishing a sword. "Wait a minute. Let me take that back."

Julie laughed along with the others and then concentrated on her food for a while. She felt happy and hungry and filled with eager anticipation to see Matt again. She just wished she wasn't the recipient of so many inquiring stares. "Everyone seems surprised to see me here," she remarked after a moment. "Was there someone else or—"

"There was a girl last season, but apparently she was more interested in spending his money than sharing his life. I didn't know her very well. She kept to herself or brought her own friends."

"So I'm this season's girl." She couldn't help the note of cynicism in her voice.

"I hope you'll last longer than that."

"I just wish Matt didn't have such a reputation."

"That's all it is—a reputation."

"I don't know." Julie shook her head in confusion. "I've heard so many stories, I don't know what to believe. Sometimes I think baseball players have their own set of ethics."

Connie was clearly taken aback by her statement, and Julie wished she had phrased her thought more carefully.

"I hope you're not including my husband in that."

"No, I'm sorry. Actually I was thinking of someone else. A player that really was everything the press said he was, and more." She paused as Connie's eyes narrowed thoughtfully. "My father was Jack Michaels."

"The pitcher?"

"Yes. I guess you've heard of him."

"Who hasn't? So that's the reason for all these suspicions. I had a feeling there was something deep troubling you. But Matt never said anything, and I didn't connect your name. Michaels is rather common."

"Matt didn't want me to feel like I had to answer a lot of questions about my past, that's why he didn't tell you. I just wanted you to know that I wasn't maligning your husband, just trying to rid myself of some bad memories."

"I don't know much about your father other than recognizing the name, but I guess he didn't live up to your expectations."

"No, but perhaps they were too high. I'm beginning to think I should have treated him more like a father and less like my hero. Maybe then he wouldn't have had so far to fall."

Connie nodded, her eyes filled with understanding and compassion. "I don't know what it was like to grow up with baseball, but I do know what it's like to be involved as a grown woman. These guys can be difficult to deal with, and I've had my share of jealous moments, especially when I was younger. But thankfully Gary's ego trip didn't last much beyond the first hitting slump. Then the glamour, money and prestige faded away, and he realized this was going to be a very difficult job. He's a good man. I wouldn't trade him for anything, except—'' she looked at her watch with a sigh ''—except for perhaps a faster dresser. Oh, there they are now.''

The women set down their plates as Matt and Gary walked in along with several other players. Julie stood up, feeling a sudden nervous tingle down her spine as she met his eyes. There was a mixture of pride and happiness in his look as he reached out to give her a hug. She clung to him for just a moment, enjoying the feel of his arms around her, the fragrant smell of pine soap clinging to his freshly washed skin.

''Hi,'' he said, as they pulled apart. ''I'm glad you came.''

Julie flushed at the intensity in his gaze, her doubts vanishing at the look of desire in his eyes. ''So am I.''

''How did I do tonight?''

''Didn't the press give you enough compliments?'' she teased.

''Who cares about the press? I want to know what you think.''

''Not bad.''

''Good. Let's get out of here.''

''Not so fast,'' Connie interjected. ''We're going to make our little announcement over drinks at Jack's Steak House. Can you join us? I understand if you can't.''

Matt hesitated. ''What do you think?''

Julie looked at her watch and inwardly sighed. It was almost eleven; a few drinks and then it would be midnight, and she had to work in the morning. She plastered a smile on her face. "Sounds like fun."

In the parking lot behind the steak house, Matt pulled his Ferrari into the empty space next to Julie's Honda. They had decided to take their own cars, so that Julie could leave directly from the restaurant. "Are you sure you want to do this?"

"I don't think I'll make it a long evening, but I would like to go for a few minutes. It feels strange to be a part of this scene again, although it's much different now that I'm older. Sometimes I get the craziest feeling of déjà vu, but I'm trying to let go of the past."

"Good, because I intend to make the future so good, the past will be a very, very distant memory."

"You're definitely not short on confidence."

"Not when I want something badly enough." He looked up at the neon light flashing the symbols of steak and beer overhead. "I wish we could be alone for a few minutes."

"I know, but Connie has been so nice to me, I would really feel bad if I didn't go in and toast their new baby."

"You're right, of course." He put a hand on her shoulder as she started to walk toward the door, and she looked at him in surprise. "Not so fast. I need one kiss before we go in."

"Someone might come by."

He took one sweeping glance around the empty parking lot and then leaned over and kissed her lovingly on the lips. It was meant to be a brief kiss, but his mouth touched off an immediate response in her, quelling the doubts she had been harboring about their future, telling her how deeply attracted he was to her. She gave in for a moment, wanting to show him what she couldn't yet bring herself to say.

"Break it up, Kingsley," a male voice interjected as they pulled apart.

Julie flushed under the appraisal of a pair of very blue eyes. Buddy Jackson was not alone, but the look he gave Julie was incredibly direct. Embarrassment turned to disgust.

"Jackson," Matt acknowledged, "this is Julie Michaels. Buddy Jackson."

"Nice to meet you," Buddy replied. "This is Stephanie."

The other girl looked down at Julie and smiled provocatively at Matt. "Hi, Matt."

"Stephy," he acknowledged briefly, giving her a cool smile.

Julie frowned at his casual nickname, but Matt pulled her inside the restaurant before she had time to comment. The group was gathered in the back room, and their late arrival met with scattered applause and pointed comments, sending another rush of red to her cheeks. She could see that she was going to have to develop a thicker skin.

"They're here," Gary announced unnecessarily, drawing added attention by hitting his spoon against the edge of his beer bottle. "Now we have an announcement to make." He pulled Connie close to him. "We're going to have a baby."

Their announcement sparked off a round of congratulations, and as Connie and Gary accepted hugs and handshakes, Julie felt her defenses weaken again. These people were nice. With the possible exception of

Buddy Jackson and the infamous Stephanie, the group gathered in the back room of the restaurant could have been any mix of friends. Dressed casually in jeans and sweaters, most of them looked very ordinary. The guys sitting around the table drinking beer seemed completely removed from the stoic-faced men who had taken to the field with a crowd of thirty thousand people watching their every move.

"What would you like to drink?" Matt asked in her ear. "I'll see if I can get you something from the bar."

"Beer will be fine."

"Are you sure? You don't have to go along with the crowd."

"I like beer, but make it a lite."

"Coming right up."

As Matt made his way to the bar, Julie moved to the edge of the room, content to sit on the sidelines and watch the festivities. Connie was really the only woman she knew well enough to talk to, and at the moment she was the center of attention and loving every minute of it. But then Connie was well suited to this kind of life. She was gregarious and outgoing and obviously a devoted wife with no hang-ups about baseball. She was fortunate enough to be able to do something she enjoyed—writing—and at the same time support Gary in the way that he needed. She wasn't sure that she could do the same for Matt.

Although she wasn't shy, it took her a while to make really close friends, and she didn't think she would have much in common with these women. She tended to be rather serious at times, concerned with deep problems that most people simply acknowledged. She wanted her life to make a difference. She couldn't imagine an existence of baseball games and nothing else, but she was trying to be fair, to recognize the fact that the ballplayers did contribute in other ways.

Another instinctive step back put her in the corner, and she didn't move, content to be just a shadow for the time being. Deep down, the rationalizations all boiled down to one thing, her fear of ending up like her mother. She was afraid to give up her own life for a man and then be left with nothing if things didn't work out.

"So you're Matt's latest," Stephanie drawled, coming to stand next to her. Her eyes ran up and down Julie's trim figure appraisingly.

Julie turned in surprise. She had been so caught up in her thoughts she hadn't been paying any attention to the rest of the party. Matt was still in line at the bar and Connie was somewhere in the middle of a large group of women, leaving her alone with Stephanie.

"Did he leave you already?" Stephanie asked spitefully.

"Pardon me?"

"Matt. He's a great guy, very sexy, wonderful kisser," Stephanie commented, her eyes fixed on Matt and Gary talking at the bar. "Buddy is nothing like him."

Julie gave her a cool smile, ignoring the knot in her stomach. "Is there a point to this?"

Stephanie smiled derisively as she gave Julie a long, sweeping glance. "I give you two weeks, tops, and then I'll be waiting." She walked away, leaving Julie blustering with anger.

"Julie?" Connie asked hesitantly, appearing unexpectedly at her side.

"What?" she snapped, her frown fading as she saw it was Connie and not another obnoxious woman.

"Sorry, I just had a very unpleasant conversation with Miss February."

"I saw."

"So did I," Matt said quietly, as he and Gary walked over to join them. "Why don't we call it a night."

Julie nodded. "Yes, I'm sorry to run out on you, but I'm exhausted."

"Don't worry about it. Will I see you tomorrow?" Connie asked. "It's the last home game before they leave for Chicago."

"I guess I should get a schedule," Julie said.

"You can decide later." Matt put a possessive arm around her shoulders. "See you two tomorrow."

After exchanging goodbyes with the rest of the group, Matt and Julie were finally alone again in the quiet parking lot. "Did Stephanie say something to bother you?" Matt asked as Julie fiddled with her keys.

"It's not important."

"There's nothing between us. If she said something to the contrary, it's just not true."

"Okay."

"Do you really mean that? You believe me?"

"Yes. I don't have any reason to doubt you."

He let out a long sigh of relief, drawing a smile to her lips.

"Not yet, anyway," she added half seriously.

"I'll tell you anything you want to know about my life," he offered. "No more secrets between us, right?"

Julie shook her head. "Thanks, but I don't think the middle of a parking lot a few minutes before midnight is the perfect time for exchanging confidences."

His green eyes sparkled down at her in the moonlight. "You're right. I tend to be a night person during the season. The adrenaline gets going so high during a game that it takes a few hours to come down."

"I'm not a night person, Matt. My day starts at seven, and I need my sleep. I have no idea how I'm going to handle this kind of a schedule," she said abruptly, throwing her purse onto the passenger seat.

"Well, let's just break it off right now then, Julie," he said in mock despair. "How will we ever make it?"

She shook her head with a frown. "I also get grumpy when I get tired."

Matt put his hands on her shoulders and looked down into her eyes, that same tender look on his face, the one that caught at her heart. "I have to go," she said softly.

"Okay. Just don't keep throwing obstacles in our way. Let's tackle one problem at a time."

"Fine. My problem right now is lack of sleep."

"Good night," he said hastily, pulling her up against his chest. "But I can't go to sleep without this." The kiss was far too short and much too public, but for the moment it would have to do.

"Good night, Matt." She slid into her seat and paused, rolling down her window, as he started to walk to his car. "You don't have to follow me home. It's out of the way."

He waved her excuse away. "Don't worry about it."

She opened her mouth to protest and gave up as he got into his car and slammed the door. Matt Kingsley liked to get his own way. She smiled to herself as she pulled out of the parking lot. It wasn't such a bad quality.

"Crisis time," Angela announced, poking her head into Julie's office just before three o'clock the next afternoon. "The flyers for the walkathon came back from the printer with a typographical error. Bob wants something done immediately. They're supposed to go out tomorrow. I can't go, because I have to chair the board meeting in an hour. Can I beg you to handle it?"

Julie made a face and looked down at her own stack of work in dismay. "I'll do it, but we are definitely switching printers after this."

"Good luck. Monty's Speed Press is the only printer that gives a sixty percent discount for nonprofit."

"That's because he does a sixty percent job."

"Agreed, but what can we do?"

"I don't know. Today has been one frustration after another." She rolled her neck around, rubbing the tired muscles as Angela departed with a commiserating wave. Sighing, she reached for her keys and then paused as the phone caught her eye. Debating her options, she finally picked up the receiver. She first dialed Matt's home only to get his answering machine. After leaving a brief message that she would try to call him about the game, she dialed the Cougars. Stonewalled once again, she had to be content with another message asking Matt to call her if he got a chance. Then she picked up her purse and set off to do battle with the printers.

By the time she finished with Monty it was nearly five, and the traffic going downtown to the wharf was horrendous. She had barely gotten through the office door when Angela pulled her into the board meeting to discuss the latest concerns over budgeting and hiring more staff. Six o'clock passed and then seven, and as the clock ticked relentlessly toward game time, Julie was swamped with guilt. When the meeting finally broke up at seven-thirty she walked into her office and faced a stack of messages from Matt with a sinking heart.

"That was quite a session," Angela remarked, following her into the office. "I had no idea the rent on this building was so high or that our insurance had nearly tripled. It's a shame how much we have to spend on overhead when there are so many problems we need to address." She paused as her eyes caught the clock. "You're late for the game."

Julie sighed. "I know, but I couldn't exactly get up in the middle of the meeting and go to a baseball game. The season is only three days old, and I'm already running into problems. There's no way I can work all day and run to a ball game every night."

"Who says you have to?"

"No one, I suppose. But you know how it is in the beginning of a relationship. You want to be there for the other person. You want to share everything. I want to go to his games. I really do."

"You don't have to convince me."

"Maybe I'm trying to convince myself."

"Talk to Matt. He probably doesn't expect you to come to every game, just enough to show you care."

Julie smiled hopefully. "Maybe you're right. But it's hard to see the other women going every night, always there offering support and encouragement. Matt probably wants and needs that, too."

"Most of those women don't work."

"I know. I just wish I could have reached him before the game. I hope he got my message."

"He'll understand," Angela offered with a consoling smile. "He has a demanding job, and so do you. Just talk to each other. It will work out in the end."

"Thanks for the pep talk. I still think you missed your calling by not going into counseling."

Angela laughed. "I'm afraid I'm too much of a busybody. I like to voice my opinions rather than remain completely objective. Not a very good trait for a counselor."

"No, but a good one for a friend."

"Go home, get some rest and don't even think about taking any work with you," Angela advised, walking out of the office.

Julie stared at the pile of messages and her half-written press release. Ignoring Angela's advice, she decided to take the time to get organized—it would mean less work for the morning.

By the time she got home it was nearly ten and after fixing herself a light snack, she sat down to catch the evening sports edition on the television. But sometime between the weather and sports, she drifted asleep and missed the startling news story at the Cougars game.

Chapter Ten

The harsh ring of the telephone interrupted a lovely dream about Matt, and Julie reached first for her clock and then for the light, groaning as she saw that the dial read 6:10. She still had twenty minutes before she had to get up. If it wasn't an emergency, she was going to kill the person on the other end.

"Hello." Her eyes flew open. "Is that you, Matt?"

"Yeah. I don't know if you heard the news, but I wanted to call you myself and tell you it's nothing serious."

"Nothing serious," she repeated. "What are you talking about? Where are you?"

"I'm at home. I wanted to catch you before you left for work, and I wasn't sure what time you got up."

She shook her head in confusion, trying to clear the sleep out of her eyes. "Did something happen?"

"You didn't hear it on the news?" he countered slowly.

Was there a hidden accusation in his tone or was it her own feeling of guilt? "No, last night was crazy. I didn't get home from work until nearly ten and then I tried to stay up, but I guess I fell asleep. What happened?"

"I got hit by a pitch, a high fastball thrown by Jimmy Davis. It took me down for the count," he said dryly. "I have a mild concussion, but nothing is broken. I just didn't want you to worry. I didn't know if you had heard."

"No, if I had, I would have called you or found you," she said tensely. "I had no idea. I feel terrible that I didn't know."

"Hey, I didn't call to make you feel guilty. I just wanted to update you on my condition. I'm fine, really. I was only out for about ten seconds, and they observed me for a few hours, and now I'm fine."

"Are you sure? Did you go to the hospital?"

"For a couple of hours. But other than a blinding headache, I'm still as hardheaded as ever."

"Don't joke. I'm sure you must feel awful."

"I've felt better." He paused. "But I don't want to discuss this. I really called because I wanted to talk to you, and my plane leaves at six o'clock tonight. I was wondering if we could get together today, and I also wanted to make sure you didn't miss the game because you were upset about something."

"No, it was work. I tried to call. Didn't you get my message?"

"Yeah, but when I called you back, your receptionist told me you weren't available."

"Now you know how I feel. The Cougars aren't exactly receptive to phone calls for you." Her voice trailed off as she thought about the demands of their jobs. She wished she could throw everything aside and spend the day with him, but she had a volunteer workshop to run at eleven and a hundred other details to take care of.

"Are you still there?" he asked, breaking into the silence.

"I'm sorry, Matt. I don't think I can meet you today."

"Don't worry about it," he said lightly, trying not to let the hurt show in his voice. He wanted some tender, loving care, and in his beat-up state he wasn't thinking clearly. Of course she was busy, and there was nothing wrong with him that a few hours' rest wouldn't cure. "I guess I'll see you on Monday. We come back late Sunday night. Monday is a free day and then we'll be playing at home for the next ten days."

Julie listened as he rattled off the schedule for the next few weeks. Despite his joking manner, she sensed he was not quite up to his usual self. His lightheartedness was a little too forced, and she could only imagine how he would feel after getting hit in the head by a fastball.

"Well, I'll let you get to work," he said finally.

"If you need me, I'll come over," she stated, making a snap decision. "I can cook you some breakfast and make sure you're okay. I'm worried about your head. I don't think you should be alone."

The tension squeezed out of his body at the concern in her voice. "As much as I would love to have you here, I think you should probably go to work. I'm fine, and Connie said she would check in on me."

"Okay. If you're sure."

"I'm sure. Take care of yourself, Julie."

"Bye, Matt." The dial tone hummed in her ear, and she stared indecisively at the receiver. She wanted to be with him. The thought of him lying there hurt and in pain was tormenting her. He said he was fine, she reminded herself, knowing full well that Matt probably wasn't telling her the truth. And then there was work. She had commitments, responsibilities. She flopped back against the pillows in despair.

Compromise. She would have to compromise for once. She could spend the morning at work, finish the workshop and go see Matt in the afternoon. It was the best she could do.

Julie pounded the steering wheel of her car in frustration as traffic once again ground to a halt on the freeway leading out of San Francisco. It was only three o'clock—too early for rush hour, but you would never know it by the mass of cars trying to leave the city.

Her nerves were on edge from trying to pack everything she could into a few hours to get out early enough and catch Matt. He had told her he would be leaving for the airport at five. With any luck they would have at least an hour together.

Unfortunately, by the time she pulled into his driveway it was half past four. With the minutes ticking away, she hurried up to the front door and pushed down on the bell.

The sound of voices from within barely registered, and she was taken by surprise when a beautiful young woman opened the door. Julie stepped back in confusion, her eyes seeking out the number on the door.

"Can I help you?" the woman inquired.

"Who is it, Colleen?"

There was no disguising Matt's voice. Julie felt a stabbing pain in her gut.

"She hasn't said," Colleen remarked speculatively as Matt joined her from behind.

"Julie, come in. I didn't think you were going to be able to come by."

"I guess not," she said tightly, looking from one to the other.

Matt smiled into her stony expression. "Colleen is my cousin. Can you give us a minute, Colleen? I think Julie and I need to talk."

"Sure thing. I just wanted to make sure you were okay."

"Thanks for coming by and tell Aunt Jo that I appreciate the chicken soup."

Colleen looked from one to the other and then shrugged her shoulders. "Keep in touch." She picked her purse up off the hall table and walked out to her car.

"Come on in, Julie. Let's talk."

She made an apologetic gesture with her hand. "I'm sorry I snapped at you and Colleen. I had a hard time getting down here and she took me by surprise."

"I know." Matt rubbed his throbbing head with one hand, his eye on the clock over Julie's head. "I have to go in fifteen minutes. I wish we had more time."

"I do, too," she murmured. "I worked like mad to get my desk cleared so that I could come down and see you, then I hit traffic jam after traffic jam and then—"

Matt covered the distance between them and silenced her with one finger against her lips. "Don't say anything more."

"I just want you to understand that I really tried to get here," she mumbled against his fingers.

The smile on his lips matched the gleam in his green eyes. It was the last thing she saw before he lowered his head and kissed her.

His touch was filled with emotion and promise, and she clung to him, knowing that once again they would be facing time apart. Her hands locked behind his neck as she responded to his demanding mouth and the soft murmurs of endearment.

"I have to go," he said finally, watching the desire slowly fade from her eyes.

"This is harder than I thought. There never seems to be enough time." Her voice caught as her exhausted emotions threatened to spill out in a river of tears.

"It's not going to be easy," he admitted. "I've always tried to stay pretty free of relationships especially during baseball season."

"Then why do you want us to keep seeing each other?"

"Why do you think?"

Julie shook her head and took a step back. "I don't know what to think. You've turned my life upside down. I can't believe I'm involved in baseball again. My mind says this is crazy, but my heart says something completely different."

"Like what?" he asked with interest.

"Never mind. Just hold me for a minute. I'm going to need something to keep me going for the next week."

"With pleasure," he said deeply.

Their embrace was so tight, Julie could barely breathe, but she revelled in the feeling of closeness, wishing that they had more time to explore their feelings, to talk, but time moved on.

"I'll call you," Matt promised.

She nodded, wiping a smudge of lipstick off his cheek.

"And Julie, try not to worry so much. You can trust me."

* * *

Trust me, trust me, trust me. The phrase echoed through Julie's mind as she sat down to watch the sports report on the late news. Matt had been gone four days— a very long four days. He had called her twice and left messages on her answering machine, and the previous evening he had finally reached her just as she was getting ready for bed.

Their conversation had been warm and friendly. He was getting ready to leave for San Diego where the team would be playing for three days, and he was looking forward to seeing his family and inviting them to the game. He had told her he missed her, but the distance and the telephone call were more depressing than cheerful. She wanted to be with him, sharing in what was happening, but she also wanted him to be with her. She wanted to talk to him about her problems at work, about the constantly dwindling supply of volunteers. But most of all she just wanted to be in his arms.

Throughout the week she had found herself searching avidly through newspapers for mention of the Cougars, and she never missed the sports report on the evening news, usually flipping back and forth on every channel to make sure some tidbit of information didn't pass her by. But now as she waited for the ever optimistic sports reporter to begin his report, she realized that tonight's segment was a little different.

The Cougars were about to start a three-day series in San Diego, and the television crew had followed them to a team barbecue being held at the ranch house of one of the team coaches. It was a lively party and everywhere she looked there were players, wives and women.

Julie felt her heart stop as Matt came into view, looking sexily handsome in a pair of blue jeans and

plaid shirt. He wore a Stetson hat on his head in the
spirit of the barbecue and a pair of cowboy boots, and
she had never seen a man look so good.

The reporter caught up with Matt, and asked him
what it felt like to play in his hometown and asked a few
baseball questions that he answered in his usual cheerful fashion, but there was no mention of anything personal, and he disappeared quickly back into the crowd.
Julie stared at the tiny television, swearing under her
breath when the camera zoomed in on the reporter,
eliminating most of the background action. She had
wanted to see more of Matt, more of what was happening, but the brief segment was over, and Julie
flipped off the television in disgust.

Getting up from the couch, she walked over to the
refrigerator and stared blankly at the unappetizing dis-
play of food. It was dinnertime, but she wasn't hungry.
She was just about to close the door when her eyes
caught sight of the package of hot dogs she seemed to
keep buying, and the inevitable bowl of chili she kept
cooking. If she couldn't have Matt, at least she could
relive some memories.

"He's back," Angela announced as Julie walked in
late Thursday afternoon. "Matt called you at least five
times today."

"What did he say?"

"Nothing too personal, just that he desperately wants
to see you. I've always liked that quality in a man. It
sounds so romantic, desperate."

"Matt tends to exaggerate. Did he leave a number?"

"Three." Angela handed her a stack of pink slips.
"But since it is now after four, I would suggest you read

the last message that states that he is going to pick you up at five o'clock.''

"That's in fifteen minutes," Julie wailed. "I can't leave. I have to write a summary of today's fund-raising tour before the board meeting tomorrow."

Angela looked at her in disbelief. "The board meeting isn't until three, and the report doesn't have to be anything fancy. Do it tomorrow."

"I suppose I could."

"Just do it, Julie. You only live once. It might as well be interesting."

"That's one thing Matt definitely is—interesting. Did he happen to mention where we were going?"

"No, but it probably doesn't matter, does it?"

Julie shook her head. "You are terrible."

"No, just envious. He sounds like a wonderful guy. Ask him if he has a brother."

"He has two as a matter of fact. But they live in San Diego."

"Just my luck."

"Sorry," Julie said with a laugh. "I better try to get something done before he comes."

Angela sighed and went back to her own desk. Julie sat down and tried to concentrate on summarizing her day, but Matt's lazy, teasing grin kept popping up before her eyes. She had never thought she would miss him so much. She just hoped they could spend a quiet evening together, preferably alone. They hadn't had the luxury of time in quite a while. But Matt had other ideas.

His arrival at her office was met with an appreciative round of applause from Angela and the receptionist, and Julie jerked to her feet at the mention of his name. Before she could move the door opened. The look in his eyes made her catch her breath, but his sleek, black tuxedo made her heart stop. She stared at him in amazement.

"Hello, sweetheart," he said with a grin, pulling a dozen red roses from behind his back.

"You're crazy."

"About you." He handed her the flowers. "I hope you like red."

She took the offering with a bemused smile. "I don't know what to say. You've taken me completely by surprise. I thought we were just going to get a bite to eat somewhere."

"We are. I have the entire evening planned. I hope you aren't busy. I tried to call, but I couldn't get you on the phone." His tone grew more serious. "I want to have a special evening with you."

She swallowed convulsively. "I'd like that, too, but where are we going? We certainly don't match," she added, looking down at her plain navy-blue skirt and blazer.

"Don't worry about that. We can stop at your place on our way to dinner."

"Where are we going?"

"It's a surprise."

"Come on, just a little hint."

"No way. Are you ready to go or do you need a few minutes?"

"Two minutes," she said with an eager smile. "Just let me put this stuff back together and then I'll be ready."

"I'll meet you downstairs."

"What's going on?" Angela demanded, pushing her way into the office as soon as Matt had left.

"He's taking me out."

"Those roses are gorgeous. Spectacular."

Julie looked down at the enormous bouquet and then back into her friend's eyes. "He's a pretty nice guy, isn't he?"

"Do you have to ask? Go on, get out of here, before I steal him away from you."

Julie laughed and grabbed her purse out of the desk drawer. She slipped one rose out of the bouquet and handed the rest back to Angela. "Can you take care of these for me?"

"No problem. They'll look great on my desk," Angela called as Julie ran out of the office.

Matt was waiting downstairs, standing next to a long white stretch limousine that was double-parked in front of their building and already arousing a great deal of curiosity. Julie felt like a celebrity, and then she smiled at her own foolish thoughts. Matt was the celebrity, not her.

She stopped just a few inches away from him, her heart pounding against her chest as she looked into his eyes. "I'm ready."

He stared at her for a long moment, with an intensity that was so distant from his usual playfulness. "It's good to see you again."

"You, too," she whispered. "I missed you."

He took a deep breath and then opened the car door. "Why don't you hop in, so I can show you how much I missed you."

"I'd love to." She slid into the elegant, plush interior and stared in amazement at the fully stocked bar and romantic lighting. "This is incredible. You're spoiling me."

"Good." He reached for her and everything else slipped from her mind as his lips touched her mouth.

He was warm and then hot, his mouth demanding and persuading and promising all at the same time. She moved closer, burying her fingers in the soft curls of his hair, pressing her breasts against his tuxedo jacket until she felt a deep ache for his touch on her skin.

It was Matt who finally pulled away, taking several long, deep breaths as he put a little distance between them. "If we don't stop now, you're never going to get dinner."

"I'm not complaining," she murmured.

"Neither am I, believe me." He paused as he straightened his jacket. "But I have a very special evening planned, and everything in due time." He reached for the bottle of champagne and poured her a glass. "First, a toast."

She accepted the glass reluctantly, preferring the taste of Matt's touch to the taste of champagne. "What shall we drink to?"

"To you. A very special lady and what I hope will be a very special night."

They clinked their glasses in mutual accord, desire dancing back and forth between their eyes.

"Don't tempt me, Julie," he warned as she stared longingly at his mouth.

She smiled and then sat back on her seat. "Then tell me what we're doing tonight."

"It's a secret. You'll just have to wait and see."

"You didn't have to go to all this trouble."

"It's no trouble, and to tell you the truth I have an underlying purpose."

"What's that?"

"I've been thinking a lot about my life the past few days, and I know that my fame has caused a few problems for you, for both of us. It never bothered me before. I guess, because the women I've dated in the past have been thrilled to be part of the spotlight. But you're different.''

''Is that good or bad?''

''Definitely good. That's why tonight I want to show you the flip side. Fame and money can cause a lot of problems, but sometimes, every once in a while, they can be fun.''

''That sounds interesting. Tell me more.''

He laughed out loud—a rich tone that warmed her soul. ''I have a lot of money, Julie. I've never been one to throw it around. I guess my mother's conservative values are just too deeply ingrained. But once in a while, I figure, what the hell, live a little.'' He paused, the tender light returning to his eyes. ''Tomorrow begins another series of baseball, but tonight, for one special night, I think we should forget about our problems, our pasts and just concentrate on each other. What do you think?''

''I can't think of anything I'd rather do,'' she said softly.

''Then sit back and relax, because tonight is just for you.''

Chapter Eleven

They finished another glass of champagne as the limousine moved swiftly through the streets of San Francisco. Their stop at Julie's apartment was brief. She changed into the sexiest dress she could find—a slinky black silk with a plunging neckline that made a perfect foil for her golden hair.

Within the hour they were crossing the Golden Gate Bridge, caught up in the romantic twilight. She was almost sorry when the car stopped, but Matt's eyes twinkled with anticipation as he got out of the car and extended his hand. They were parked next to the Sausalito boat harbor with not a restaurant in sight.

"Where are we?" she asked curiously.

He put a finger to her lips and smiled. "You'll see. Follow me." He led her down the pier and finally up the steps to a very large yacht where they were met by an older man in uniform.

"Captain Donovan," Matt greeted him with a smile, shaking his hand. "This is Julie Michaels."

"Hello," she said politely.

"Is everything ready?"

Captain Donovan nodded complacently. "Yes, sir. Please go inside, make yourselves comfortable. We'll be leaving within a few moments."

"Great." He turned to Julie. "Are you coming?"

She looked at Matt in amazement and then preceded him into a large, lovely salon. She had never been on a yacht before and was astonished at the spaciousness of the room. There were two long couches set under several portholes and in one corner there was an intimate table for two complete with silverware and flowers. The entire room was lighted with candles and there was a soft background of music.

"I'm impressed," she said lightly. "Beneath all that strutting and spitting tobacco lurks a romantic heart."

"I never spit," he retorted with a grin. "Strutting, maybe just a little when I hit a home run."

"Seriously, this is beautiful. It's like a fantasy." She turned to the porthole as the muffled roar of the engine started their sail. Within minutes the yacht had moved effortlessly into the San Francisco Bay. The sky was dusky twilight, the stars just beginning to make their appearance and in the distance the night lights of San Francisco came on one by one. She didn't think she had ever seen a more beautiful sight.

Matt came up quietly behind her, placed his arms around her waist and pulled her back against his chest.

"It's beautiful."

"No, you're beautiful," he whispered, landing a teasing kiss on her neck.

"Is it just the two of us?" she asked, suddenly aware of the intimacy of their surroundings.

"There's a crew of four, but otherwise we're alone. I thought about taking you to a really exclusive restaurant, but it seemed too public. I wanted to have something extraordinary but also private. The yacht was the only thing I could think of."

"Is it yours?"

"No. It belongs to a friend of mine." His arms tightened around her waist. "I can't believe we're finally alone."

She leaned back against him, reveling in the warm strength of his arms and the solid chest supporting her. His lips touched the corner of her ear in an erotic gesture that sent a tingle through every nerve in her body.

"Matt," she whispered so softly that he bent his head to hear her. "Kiss me again."

His eyes turned jade at her request and slowly he bent his head, brushing her mouth teasingly and then deepening the kiss until she was breathless.

"How was that?" he asked teasingly.

"Not bad."

"What do you mean—" His reply was interrupted by the beep of the intercom. "Saved by the bell."

Julie smiled as he exchanged words with the steward.

"Dinner will now be served," he said, waving her toward the intimate table for two.

"We're not having hot dogs and chili, are we?"

"I know it's your favorite, Julie."

"Please tell me it's not hot dogs and chili."

"We're having lobster and steak with vegetables, rice, salad, soup, and whatever you want for dessert."

"That sounds wonderful." Her eyes opened wide as two uniformed waiters entered with the first course, a shrimp salad, sitting resplendent on a silver tray. It was the beginning of the most sumptuous feast she had ever tasted.

The evening was absolutely perfect, Julie thought later, as they took a stroll along the deck after dinner. Matt had draped his jacket around her for warmth, and she loved the feel of his coat around her almost as much as she loved the way his arm hugged her against his waist. They stopped for a moment to gaze out at the view. The bay was quiet, as the yacht made its way gracefully through the water. Standing under the moon and the stars, Julie could hear the sound of their breathing, as the desire that had been simmering between them all evening suddenly caught fire.

By mutual accord they turned into each other's arms, her mouth seeking his, their lips parting as the kiss deepened and their passion intensified. The kisses seemed to go on forever—long, slow, drugging kisses that never seemed to be enough.

"Let's go inside," Matt muttered, raising his head long enough to pull her back into the main salon. Immediately his mouth was on hers, his hands shedding the coat from her back, his fingers trailing sensuously down her bare shoulders.

Julie was filled with an irrepressible need to get closer to him, and her fingers flew down the front of his shirt, unbuttoning and pulling the material out of his pants. She wanted to touch him more intimately, and she sighed with satisfaction when her fingers found his bare skin. The muscles stiffened beneath her caress, and she reveled for a moment in her own power, but then he pulled her over to the couch and down onto the soft cushions.

He slipped the strap off her shoulder so his lips could caress her neck, taste her skin as he pulled the dress down to reveal the soft fullness of her breast.

Her breath caught at his intimate kiss, and she closed her eyes, burying her hands in the curly strands of his hair, holding him close as his kisses created a burning need within her. "You're driving me crazy," she murmured.

He brought his lips to her mouth, satisfying and tantalizing at the same time. Finally, he pulled away, his eyes deadly serious. "I want to make love to you, Julie."

Her heart raced at his words, but the distance between them, the lingering question in the air made her hesitate. Why had he stopped? Why was he giving her a chance to pull back? She didn't want to think, she just wanted to feel.

The air crackled between them and after a long moment, Matt moved away, pulling her into a sitting position next to him and gently pushing the straps of her dress back into place.

She stared at him in confusion. "I'm sorry."

He shook his head. "Don't apologize."

"I want to explain."

"No, you're right. It's too soon." He jerked to his feet so quickly she wondered if he wasn't having second thoughts himself.

"Matt?"

"Do you want a drink?" he asked, striding over to the bar and pouring himself a shot of vodka.

"No."

He drained the glass and stared fixedly out of the porthole.

"What are you thinking?" she asked hesitantly, bewildered by the sudden awkward silence between them.

"I'm thinking that—that it's late, and we should probably head back. I'll let the captain know."

Julie expelled a long sigh as he left. She took a moment to pull her dress back into order, and wished she could straighten out her life just as easily.

He returned within a few minutes, his face clearer and his eyes resolute. "We're going to head to shore now. The limo will take you back to your house and pick you up again in the morning, so you won't have to bother collecting your car tonight."

"Sounds like you've thought of everything."

His smile was somewhat derisive. "I thought I had."

"This has been a wonderful evening," she said softly, as he sat down stiffly on the other end of the couch. "It was like a fantasy, only better because it was real."

"I'm glad."

Julie clasped her hands nervously in her lap, playing with the tiny ring on her finger and wishing she knew what to say to bring back the closeness they had had before.

After a long moment, Matt let out a breath and then shook his head. "Look, I don't want to ruin this evening. I wanted it to be something special, a little time away from the schedules. I certainly didn't bring you here to seduce you, although I must admit the thought crossed my mind once or twice."

"Mine, too. I guess I wasn't as ready as I thought."

He nodded his head in what she assumed was agreement, but he remained oddly silent. After a moment he moved across the couch to sit next to her. He threw an arm around her shoulders and pulled her head down on his chest. "Let's just enjoy the rest of our sail. The future will take care of itself."

She closed her eyes and hoped he was right.

The next few weeks passed in a dream. There were a few cozy dinners, a lot of late-night suppers and even a couple of devastating kisses, but the demands of both their jobs prohibited them from talking too deeply about the future. They were taking it one day at a time.

As spring turned into summer, the Cougars went on a long road trip and Julie attended to the endless details involved in her next big event, a walkathon spanning four counties. Her attendance at the home games began to dwindle, and although Matt carefully avoided adding any pressure, she could see the dissatisfaction in his eyes and hear the disappointment in his voice when they talked about their conflicting schedules.

It wasn't enough for either of them. Something was going to have to give, and things finally came to a head when Julie returned to her apartment late on Tuesday night with a throbbing headache and a briefcase of work to be tackled before the morning. She was just about to open the door to her building when a hand came down on her shoulder.

"Julie."

"Matt? You scared me to death."

"Sorry." He dropped his hand.

"What are you doing here? The game can't be over yet." She looked at her watch. It was only ten, and then her eyes ran down his body. He was wearing jeans and a sweatshirt, his face was stubbly with a day's growth of beard and his eyes had a strange, eerie light in them.

"It's not." He took the key from her hand and opened the door and they walked silently up the stairs to her apartment.

Once they were inside she turned back to face him. "What happened?"

"Why didn't you come tonight?"

She swallowed nervously. "I called and left a message. Didn't they tell you? I had a crisis at work. I couldn't leave. I tried, but I couldn't get away."

"But you knew tonight was important."

"Your anniversary with the team," she said slowly, feeling a stabbing guilt.

"So you did remember." He sat down on the sofa and leaned his head on his hands.

"Of course I remembered. I just couldn't get away. But why are you here? Why aren't you playing?"

"I got thrown out. I picked a fight with the umpire and he tossed me. I'll probably be fined for walking out before the game ended, but to hell with it."

Julie sat next to him on the sofa, frightened by his extreme coldness, the anger in his voice.

"I wasn't yelling at the umpire. I was yelling at you," he said flatly. "I wanted you to be there tonight. You let me down."

"I'm sorry. The walkathon is only four days away. I have responsibilities. Five of my key volunteers walked out on me today. I wouldn't have missed this game if I'd had a choice. I wish you would believe that."

"Oh, hell, I don't know what to believe anymore."

She studied him thoughtfully. "Are we still talking about the game or is something else bothering you?"

He looked at her for a long moment. "Did you know your father was going to toss out the ball tonight?"

Her heart plummeted into her stomach as she stared back at him.

"That's what I thought."

"But that's not why I missed the game."

"Isn't it, Julie? You can blame work or a hundred other things, but it always comes back to your father. Every time we start to get really close, you back away. Deep down you still think I'm just like your father, don't you?"

"No," she cried. "That's not true. I missed the game because my job is important to me. It has nothing to do with my father."

"I don't think you wanted to see him. I think you used work as an excuse. But what hurts the most is that you just didn't tell me how you felt."

"Okay, I admit I had qualms about seeing him again. But I wasn't going to let it stop me from coming to the game. I thought I was ready to face him again."

"But you chickened out."

She sighed and got to her feet, then began pacing restlessly around the room. Was he right? Had she used work as a crutch? "Maybe," she said finally. "Maybe you're right. But it wasn't a conscious decision. I really did have an emergency. My job is important to me just like baseball is important to you."

"You're going to have to face him someday, and the sooner the better. I have to know."

"Know what?" she asked in bewilderment.

"I have to know if you're ever going to be able to really trust me, to tell me how you feel."

"And what about you?" she said slowly. "You haven't said the words, either."

His jaw tightened and the pulse in his throat beat mercilessly as he stared into her questioning eyes. "I don't know if I can choose between you and baseball, and that's what you want, isn't it?''

She turned her back on him, grappling with her own feelings. ''I'm not asking you to make a choice, but you seem to be asking me to make one.''

''This isn't just about our careers, Julie. This is about us, and it still comes back to your father. Until you resolve your feelings about the way he left you, we're never going to be able to tear down this wall between us.''

''Do you really want to?''

He looked at her for a long time and then slowly nodded. ''More than anything.''

Julie spent the next few days arguing with her conscience and her heart. She didn't want to admit that her father's presence at the ball game had had anything to do with her missing the game. But deep down, she thought she was probably lying to herself. She had solved her work problems by seven-thirty that night, but instead of running down to the ballpark, she had dawdled, convincing herself that it was too late to go and that Matt would understand. But he hadn't understood and his disappointment cut through her like a knife. She had let him down, because she was afraid.

She loved him, but she was hanging on to her job like a lifeline, using it as an excuse to keep some distance between them. She kept remembering her mother's sad face and the long weeks of loneliness after the divorce. Her mother had dedicated herself to baseball and to her father, and when that life ended, she had nothing left. It had taken her a long time to rebuild her life and watching her had been very painful. Julie had decided

then and there that she would never end up in the same
position.

But here it was, eight years later, and she was facing
a similar choice. Loving Matt was a risk she wanted to
take. But she couldn't help wondering how he really
felt. He cared about her, he was attracted to her, but he
had never said he loved her. How could she take that
final step without knowing the truth?

Unfortunately, she couldn't ask him, because he had
left for a two-night stand in Los Angeles, and she still
had the walkathon to take care of. Maybe on Saturday,
when everything was over, they could sit down and talk.
She hoped it wouldn't be too late.

The walkathon arrived on a day filled with fog and a
light rain. It was a rather depressing finale to her recent
weeks of dedicated work. But there was still a job to be
done.

In the early-morning darkness, Julie slipped a pon-
cho over her head and pulled an umbrella out of the
closet of her apartment. She was determined to make
the best of things. With any luck the fog would clear by
the time the walk started, and they would be able to host
a successful fund-raiser.

She drove her car to the start of the San Francisco
walk along the Great Highway. The fog was even
thicker near the ocean, and she wondered if anyone
would turn up. But her spirits lifted as she caught sight
of five teenagers dressed in colorful clothes. They were
smiling and laughing. They reminded her of what was
important.

By eight o'clock there were nearly four hundred and
fifty walkers braving the bad weather, and the morning
flew by as Julie and the volunteer committee sent them

on the beginning of their twenty-mile trek through the streets of San Francisco.

A mobile radio station cosponsoring the walk led the way for the first mile and then sped around the bay to the other walks going on in different counties. Throughout the morning Julie received reports, and all signs pointed toward success. She found herself feeling very emotional about the day, and she knew it had a lot to do with Matt. She had devoted herself to her job, but she was beginning to realize that there was still something missing in her life, something that only Matt could give her.

She had just begun to relax when the announcement came over the radio. Tragedy had struck.

"I have to go to her," Matt stated firmly as Dale Howard chewed thoughtfully on a wad of tobacco.

"Slow down and tell me what you're talking about. Who is her and what happened?"

"Julie," he shouted in angry confusion. "She's a friend. There's been an accident on the walkathon. I just heard it on the radio. I have to go to her."

"Is she hurt?"

"It wasn't her. It was a kid, a child. She's going to be devastated. I have to go right now."

"Look, I don't know what you're talking about, but we have a game starting in two hours, and I need you here."

"Don't count on me. This is an emergency."

"Dammit, Kingsley, this is your career we're talking about."

"No, this is my life," Matt yelled, walking out of the office. The announcement on the radio had snapped everything back into place. The doubts, the indecisions were gone. He knew what he had to do. He just hoped he would have an opportunity to do it.

The lobby of San Francisco General was filled with people ranging from families and walkers to television crews. Matt pushed his way through the room, ignoring the shouts of recognition. Julie was here somewhere. He knew she wouldn't be anywhere else.

He walked through the lobby and into the corridor and then he saw her, slumped against the wall, standing next to Angela. They were hugging each other, and he paused, not knowing what to do now that he was here.

Angela saw him first, and she released Julie, giving her a warm smile, and then Julie turned, her face streaked with tears, her golden blond hair wet from the fog and the rain.

He walked over to her as Angela departed. "Are you okay?"

His eyes searched her face with concern, and he couldn't help himself, he reached out his arms and pulled her against his chest. They stayed that way for a long, long moment, and then she pulled away.

"You heard what happened?"

He nodded. "I heard that a child was injured along the highway, that a group of kids had strayed off the walk route, or something like that."

She smiled weakly. "They were just being kids. They were tired and thought they could take a shortcut rather than just admit they wanted to stop. We have vans all along the way, so that this kind of thing doesn't happen. And one of the volunteers ran after them, but they ran faster, and then one of them, a boy of about ten, got hit by a car. It's so horrible, Matt. This walk is to help kids, not to hurt them. I feel terrible. If anything happens to that child . . .''

"Shh-shh, don't think about it right now."

"I can't think of anything else. I just wish it wasn't taking so long."

"Just try to relax and be patient. We'll wait together." He led her over to a bench along one wall, holding her as the clock ticked the minutes away.

It was over an hour before the doctor came out. He spoke to the family first and then walked to where Julie and the foundation staff were gathered. His face was kind and compassionate, but still very serious. Matt felt Julie tense under his arms, and he held on tighter, trying to infuse her with some strength.

"He has a broken leg, a couple of fractured ribs and a concussion. But at the moment, he doesn't appear to have any serious internal injuries. Our prognosis is guarded. Stable but guarded," the doctor said. "I would appreciate it if one of you would pass that message on to the press. I want to get back to him as soon as possible."

Robert and Angela immediately exited into the lobby as the clamor for information began.

Julie let out a long breath. "Thank God for miracles."

"He's going to be okay."

She looked into Matt's face for the first time, noticing the lines of weariness under his eyes, and the absence of his smile. She missed his smile more than anything else. "I'm glad you came."

"I am, too." He hugged her again, and as she moved into his arms, her eyes drifted to the clock. "Matt, you have a game today. It starts in half an hour. You better go."

"Not until I'm sure you're okay and that you don't need me anymore."

She smiled weakly. She was always going to need him. "I'll be fine. I need to get back to work, try to salvage something out of this day. It has been so disappointing."

"I know how hard you've worked."

"Not just me. Everyone. But thank you for coming, for caring." Her voice broke, and she blinked back the tears. "I'm feeling kind of emotional right now, I guess."

"You have a right. It's been a tough day."

"It's been a tough couple of days," she said, pulling out of his arms. "You better go. If you hurry, you can still make the game."

"I'm sure they've replaced me by now," he said with disinterest. "I've never missed a game in my life for any reason other than dire illness. They're just going to have to give me a break this time."

She shook her head in amazement. "You'd do that for me?"

"Why do you sound so surprised?" he asked wearily. "You don't have to answer that. It always comes back to your father."

"Matt, please don't start this now. We need to talk, but this isn't the time or the place." She motioned toward the waiting press, the volunteers and walkers clamoring in the outer room.

"I don't think it's ever going to be the right time or the right place. It's up to you, Julie. When you're ready, and I mean really ready, then we'll talk." He leaned over and kissed her on the cheek—a gesture that seemed more worrisome than comforting. "Take care of yourself." With that he was gone.

Chapter Twelve

Julie woke up the next morning and faced the telephone with a knot in her stomach that made her want to jump back into bed and pull the covers over her head. But it was time to stop hiding from the truth. She reached over and opened the drawer of her bedside table and pulled out her address book. Inside was her father's address and telephone number in Los Angeles. Her mother had insisted on giving it to her the day before she moved to Vancouver. Just in case you ever need to speak to him, she had said.

With a sigh, she stared heavily at his phone number, and then she picked up the phone. Each passing ring sent a shiver of trepidation and relief through her. Maybe he wouldn't be home. Maybe he had moved.

"Hello."

She recognized the deep baritone almost as if she had heard it the day before instead of eight years ago.

"Hello. Is someone there?"

"It's me. Julie," she said finally.

There was a long silence at his end. "Is that really you, baby?"

"Yes."

"I can't believe it. How are you?"

"Okay, I guess."

"Are you sure? Is everything all right?" His voice was laced with worry. "Is your mother sick or something?"

"No, she's fine, and I'm fine." She paused, and he waited for her to say why she was calling, but she didn't know where to begin. Matt had told her to resolve things with her father, but how? What could she say? What could he say that would make everything different?

"I'm glad to finally hear from you," he said quietly. "I've picked up the phone a hundred times to call you, but I was afraid you would just hang up on me."

"I probably would have," she admitted. "I wasn't ready to talk to you before, but I think I am now."

"I don't know what to say. I didn't think I'd ever hear from you again. You know I tried to see you after the divorce. I wrote you. I wrote your mother, your grandparents. No one would let me get close to you."

"They were just trying to protect me."

"I never wanted to hurt you, baby. If I could change the past, I would. Believe me I would."

"Unfortunately, you can't change what happened, and neither can I. It's taken me a long time to realize that," she replied. "Look, I know we can't do this over the phone, but I just wanted to let you know that next time you come up here, I'd like to see you. I don't know if I can ever forget what happened, but I'm trying to put it behind me."

"I'd love to see you again. Your grandmother sent me a photograph of you last year. I couldn't believe the beautiful woman you grew up to be."

Julie's eyes filled with tears at the emotion in his voice. "I have to go."

"I understand, but when can I see you?"

"Just give me a few weeks, okay? I still need a little time to sort things out."

"Whatever it takes. Just don't shut the door on me again. I love you, Julie. I always have."

Her voice caught as she said goodbye, but the tears that rolled down her face were more happy than sad. Her father loved her. She had forgotten that, too.

Three hours later, she parked her car at the baseball stadium and walked up to the Will Call window hoping that Matt had left a ticket for her. But the agent shook his head. There was no ticket today. Either Matt didn't want her there or didn't expect to see her there.

With a shrug, she bought a general admission ticket for as close to the field as she could get. Once inside, she made her way to the players' section, noticing that the seat next to Connie was now being occupied by a striking brunette—Colleen, the girl from Matt's house.

Her heart stopped. But Colleen was just his cousin, she reminded herself, and she pushed forward.

"Hi, Connie."

Connie looked at her in surprise. "I didn't know you were coming."

"I just decided."

The brunette sent her an intriguing look. "Hello, I met you at Matt's house, didn't I?"

"Yes. Colleen, isn't it? My name is Julie."

Colleen nodded. "Do you want to sit down for a minute? I want to buy a drink before the game starts."

"Thank you." Julie paused until Colleen had moved away.

"Colleen is Matt's cousin," Connie explained hastily.

"I know. I'm not worried about her, just about Matt."

"I heard about the accident yesterday. I'm sorry."

"Thanks. I guess you know that Matt missed the game to come to the hospital to be with me."

"Yes, and I was pretty impressed."

"I think it's my turn now. I want to show him that I care just as much as he does. Unfortunately, I don't think he has an open mind right now. We parted on a bad note."

"That explains his grim expression this morning."

"I want to show Matt that I'm ready to get involved in all this, more than I have in the past. Do you know what I mean?"

Connie's face lit up at her words. "Of course I know what you mean. You're in love with him, and he's in love with you. It's simple and wonderful."

"Hardly simple, and I'm not sure how he feels about me anymore," Julie said with a sad smile. "I think I might have ruined everything with all my doubts about baseball and him. But I know what I want now. I just have to prove it to him."

"What are you going to do?"

"I don't know. Do you have any ideas?"

"Why not just show him how much you care and how determined you are to get him back?"

"How do I do that?"

"There's an empty seat right behind the dugout. I know because it belongs to Margo Hughes, and she just had her baby. Why don't you borrow it for a few days? Matt can't help but see you there, and perhaps he'll get the message." She paused. "Are you sure you want to do this? I know how important your career is and that you've had a bad taste of baseball before."

"I like my job," she admitted. "But Matt is more important. And as to the bad taste in my mouth, I think it's finally gone. I really want to make this work. I know now that I never really tried before. I just complained and worried and let my fears turn into realities. But this time it's different. I plan to be here every day, every night, as long as it takes."

"Good luck."

Julie stood up as Colleen approached and offered her a brief smile. "Thanks, I think I'll need it."

She moved down to the front row, saying hello to the girl on the other side of the empty seat whom she had met just briefly, and then the game began. Matt saw her when he ran in from third in the middle of the first inning. His jog faltered for just a moment. He didn't smile or say anything, just walked into the dugout, and that was the way it was for one long week.

She got more aggressive as time went by, not content to just sit and watch. She took on studying his hitting stance and researching the pitchers he was going to be facing, and then she began to send him little notes through Connie or Gary—words of encouragement and love. He never replied, but slowly his grim look began to fade.

He never looked up into the stands or made eye contact with her, and his answering machine still took all her calls, but she managed to keep a spark of hope in her heart. If he didn't care about her, he wouldn't go to such trouble to avoid her.

But when she went to the ballpark that Friday night, she was beginning to get worried. There were only four days left of their home stand and then the team would be leaving for Chicago. She wanted something to happen before he left, and when it finally did, she had Gary to thank for it.

It was the bottom of the ninth when Gary led off the inning with the Cougars down five to three. His first two swings met air only, and his third swing sent a smashing line drive right into her seat.

The ball glanced off her shoulder with a stinging pain that barely registered as she somehow managed to catch the ball as it bounced off the top of the dugout and back into her arms. She held it up triumphantly as the crowd cheered, and in that moment in time, she knew everything had changed in her life. For ten short seconds she was a star in baseball. It was a heady, powerful feeling to be the center of attention, and as she sat down in her seat she knew she could never hate the game again.

When she looked back down on the field, Matt was watching her from the on-deck circle, and as she grinned at him a very slow smile crossed his solemn features. Then he was gone, taking his turn in the batter's box. The game went on, Matt hit a single to center field, and Julie began to feel just a little bit better. There was still hope.

When the game ended, she walked up to say good-bye to Connie.

"Nice catch," Connie commented with a smile.

"Thanks. I haven't caught a ball in years." She paused for a long moment. "That reminds me. A long time ago you asked me to play on your softball team."

"Right, and you refused."

"Any possibility there's still an opening?"

Connie nodded, her lips twisting in a wide grin. "After seeing you make that catch I definitely think we can make room for you on the team. How about to-morrow morning? We're playing a makeup game at nine o'clock."

"That sounds great."

"Good. By the way, Matt and Gary usually come to the games when they can."

Julie sent her a small smile. "Maybe we shouldn't tell anyone about this just yet."

"I had a feeling you were going to say that. Suits me fine. I can't wait to see Matt's face when you step up to the plate."

"I can't either," Julie murmured, as she made her way out of the stadium.

Saturday morning dawned with bright sunshine and a warm breeze. Julie drove down the peninsula just af-ter eight o'clock with a pack of butterflies flying around in her stomach. She had no idea why she felt so ner-vous. She was confident she could play as well as most of the women, but it had been a long time.

When she arrived at the park dressed in blue jeans and a T-shirt, she was relieved to see that the other women were dressed in similar attire and there was a general relaxed attitude among the players. Julie knew some of the women, and they made her feel welcome, especially when she volunteered to play left field.

Although Gary arrived with Connie, there was no sign of Matt, and in a way she was relieved, because facing a pitch for the first time in eight years was bothering her more than she cared to admit. Since she had met Matt, she had worked through most of the painful emotions of her past, finally coming to accept the game for what it was. This was the final step in her recovery—her own ability to walk up to the plate and play. She felt like she was going to be sick.

"You're batting fifth," Connie announced as she ran down the roster.

"Fifth?" she squeaked. "Are you sure you don't want to put me down any lower? I haven't played in years."

"Believe me, Julie, most of the women here haven't played in years and those that have— Well, just don't worry about it. I have a feeling you're going to surprise us."

Julie rolled her eyes and tried not to show her tension as the other women went up to bat. As luck would have it there were two outs when her turn came up.

When she stepped up to the plate, her instincts took over. Her right toe immediately dug out a little section of the batter's box and she shifted into her old familiar batting stance. She swung at the bat to warm up, her eyes instinctively checking the position of the fielders and when the pitcher let go of a high sailing slow pitch, Julie swung for the fence, but her swing against the slow pitch was off, and the ball tipped foul.

Connie and the others called out encouragement as she readied herself for the next pitch. Her father's voice suddenly echoed through her mind—*watch the ball, keep your weight on your back foot, swing through.* Her bat met the ball, and she ran to first base, watching the ball sail over the head of the center fielder. She rounded first, listening for instructions and then took second with all the aplomb of an experienced ballplayer. With the third-base coach waving her on, she ran to third, getting to the base just before the ball. A triple. The team cheered. Her heart sang.

She looked across the field, straight into Matt's piercing green eyes as he stood on the sidelines. He looked at her for a long moment and then tipped his hat. By the time she reached home at the end of the inning he had disappeared.

Connie's compassionate smile told her that he was gone, and she played the rest of the game with mixed feelings. She had conquered her final fear. She had finally rid herself of the bitterness and the anger. But she still hadn't gotten through to Matt.

The other women dispersed fairly rapidly at the end of the game, but Julie took her time, feeling a little depressed in spite of her victory. She was the last one to leave and when she walked into the parking lot, her step faltered.

He was waiting for her, leaning against the hood of her Honda, looking as sexy and unreachable as the first time she had seen him.

"Nice hit," he said, when she finally joined him.

"I'm glad you waited."

"Are you sure?" he asked searchingly.

"Yes. We need to talk. I'm ready now if you are."

"Go on."

She hesitated for a minute in front of his unwavering stare. He wasn't going to make this easy for her, but this time she really was ready. "I called my father last week, the morning after the walkathon, after I'd seen you at the hospital."

His eyes rounded with surprise. "You called your father?"

"You were right. It was time to put the past behind me. I don't know what will happen from here on out. I don't know if he and I can ever have a relationship again. But I've opened the door. The rest will have to come later."

"How did you feel when you talked to him?"

"Scared and then sort of sad." She squared her shoulders. "Now, it's your turn. You and I still have some unfinished business, at least I hope we do, or I've been spending a lot of time at the ballpark for nothing."

"I couldn't believe I kept seeing you game after game," he admitted. "When you caught that foul ball, the look on your face was priceless." His voice softened as a tiny smile crossed his face. "For just a minute you looked like a little girl again—happy, joyous, no hidden traumas."

"That's how I felt, Matt." Her voice filled with emotion. "I used to love baseball so much. This softball game was more than a game to me. It was a turning point—the final turning point. The bitterness is gone, the anger is gone, and it's all because of you."

He took an instinctive step forward and then stopped, his face hardening again. "Are you sure, Julie? I don't want to live in another man's shadow."

"You won't be. The shadows are all gone now. I was afraid to trust you before, afraid that I would end up like my mother, alone and unhappy. But I know that my work can never take the place of you. I love you."

His eyes lit up at the three simple words. "You've taken a hell of a long time to say that."

"And you still haven't said it," she retorted.

"That's because I was waiting for the right time, the perfect moment." He pulled her into his arms, tilting her face up so he could stare into her big beautiful eyes, eyes that were too honest and clear to hide deceit. The doubts were gone. The insecurity, the indecision had vanished. He leaned down and kissed her, his lips tasting hers with a desire that had been burning inside of him for weeks. "I love you, Julie."

A surge of joy spread through her at his touch, and she welcomed his plundering mouth, returning his kisses as if she would never be able to get enough. When his mouth left her lips to tease along her cheekbone and his tongue caressed the tender spot behind her ear, Julie moaned with delight, but it was over much too soon.

Matt pulled away again to look back into her eyes. "Why am I always kissing you in the middle of a parking lot?"

"I don't care where we are, as long as you keep on doing it."

"Believe me, I intend to. I just want you to be happy, really happy. I want to marry you, have children with you, grow old with you."

"That sounds wonderful. I wasn't sure."

"I know. I should have told you before, but I guess I had a few of my own problems to solve. I've been committed to baseball for so long that it was hard to believe that someone else was becoming more important to me. I was always afraid that someday it was going to come down to a choice between you and baseball. But the day of the walkathon when I knew you were hurting and that you needed me, I realized that the choice had already been made."

Her heart filled with joy at his words. "I don't want you to give up baseball. Not anymore. It's a part of you, an important part, and I know that you're obsessed with those shiny green diamonds. I can live with that as long as I can live with you."

"The only diamond I'm interested in right now is the one I intend to put on your finger as soon as possible."

Julie smiled up at him. "I don't want diamonds—just your heart, forever."

* * * * *

COMING NEXT MONTH

#820 PILLOW TALK—Patricia Ellis
Written in the Stars
Kendall Arden had made a big mistake in getting involved with
Jared Dalton's research on sleep. How could she confess her sensual
dreams to this oh-so-dedicated Libra man? Especially since he was the
subject of her fantasies....

#821 AND DADDY MAKES THREE—Anne Peters
Eric Schwenker firmly believed that a mother's place was at home, so why
was Isabel Mott using *his* office to care for her daughter? Maybe Isabel
could teach him about working mothers . . . and what a family truly was.

#822 CASEY'S FLYBOY—Vivian Leiber
Cautious Casey Stevens knew what she wanted—a decent, *civilized* home
for her baby. But sexy flyboy Leon Brodie tempted her to spread her wings
and fly. The handsome pilot was a good reason to let herself soar....

#823 PAPER MARRIAGE—Judith Bowen
Justine O'Malley was shocked by rancher Clayton Truscott's marriage
proposal—but then, so was he. Clayton had sworn never to trust a woman
again. But to keep his brother's children, he would do anything—
even *marry*!

#824 BELOVED STRANGER—Peggy Webb
Belinda Stubaker was incensed! Her employer, Reeve Lawrence, was
acting like Henry Higgins—insisting on teaching her the finer things in
life. How could Belinda explain to Reeve that *love* was the finest thing
there was....

#825 HOME FOR THANKSGIVING—Suzanne Carey
One kiss, so many years ago. Now, Dr. Aaron Dash and Kendra Jenkins
were colleagues at the same hospital. But that kiss could never be
forgotten. Beneath their professionalism, an intense passion
still lingered....

AVAILABLE THIS MONTH:

#814 THROUGH MY EYES
Helen R. Myers

#815 MAN TROUBLE
Marie Ferrarella

#816 DANCE UNTIL DAWN
Brenda Trent

#817 HOMETOWN HERO
Kristina Logan

#818 PATCHWORK FAMILY
Carla Cassidy

#819 EVAN
Diana Palmer

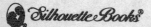

Silhouette Romance®

LONG, TALL TEXANS

EVAN
Diana Palmer

Diana Palmer's bestselling LONG, TALL TEXANS series continues with EVAN....

Anna Cochran is nineteen, blond and beautiful—and she wants Evan Tremayne. Her avid pursuit of the stubborn, powerfully built rancher had been a source of amusement in Jacobsville, Texas, for years. But no more. Because Evan Tremayne is about to turn the tables...and pursue her!

Don't miss EVAN by Diana Palmer, the eighth book in her LONG, TALL TEXANS series. Coming in September...only from Silhouette Romance.

FASHION
A WHOLE NEW YOU
WIN
CARS.TRIPS.CASH!

SILHOUETTE®
OFFICIAL SWEEPSTAKES RULES

NO PURCHASE NECESSARY

1. To enter, complete an Official Entry Form or 3" × 5" index card by hand-printing, in plain block letters, your complete name, address, phone number and age, and mailing it to: Silhouette Fashion A Whole New You Sweepstakes, P.O. Box 9056, Buffalo, NY 14269-9056.

   No responsibility is assumed for lost, late or misdirected mail. Entries must be sent separately with first class postage affixed, and be received no later than December 31, 1991 for eligibility.

2. Winners will be selected by D.L. Blair, Inc., an independent judging organization whose decisions are final, in random drawings to be held on January 30, 1992 in Blair, NE at 10:00 a.m. from among all eligible entries received.

3. The prizes to be awarded and their approximate retail values are as follows: Grand Prize — A brand-new Ford Explorer 4×4 plus a trip for two (2) to Hawaii, including round-trip air transportation, six (6) nights hotel accommodation, a $1,400 meal/spending money stipend and $2,000 cash toward a new fashion wardrobe (approximate value: $28,000) or $15,000 cash; two (2) Second Prizes — A trip to Hawaii, including round-trip air transportation, six (6) nights hotel accommodation, a $1,400 meal/spending money stipend and $2,000 cash toward a new fashion wardrobe (approximate value: $11,000) or $5,000 cash; three (3) Third Prizes — $2,000 cash toward a new fashion wardrobe. All prizes are valued in U.S. currency. Travel award air transportation is from the commercial airport nearest winner's home. Travel is subject to space and accommodation availability, and must be completed by June 30, 1993. Sweepstakes offer is open to residents of the U.S. and Canada who are 21 years of age or older as of December 31, 1991, except residents of Puerto Rico, employees and immediate family members of Torstar Corp., its affiliates, subsidiaries, and all agencies, entities and persons connected with the use, marketing, or conduct of this sweepstakes. All federal, state, provincial, municipal and local laws apply. Offer void wherever prohibited by law. Taxes and/or duties, applicable registration and licensing fees, are the sole responsibility of the winners. Any litigation within the province of Quebec respecting the conduct and awarding of a prize may be submitted to the Régie des loteries et courses du Québec. All prizes will be awarded; winners will be notified by mail. No substitution of prizes is permitted.

4. Potential winners must sign and return any required Affidavit of Eligibility/Release of Liability within 30 days of notification. In the event of noncompliance within this time period, the prize may be awarded to an alternate winner. Any prize or prize notification returned as undeliverable may result in the awarding of that prize to an alternate winner. By acceptance of their prize, winners consent to use of their names, photographs or their likenesses for purposes of advertising, trade and promotion on behalf of Torstar Corp. without further compensation. Canadian winners must correctly answer a time-limited arithmetical question in order to be awarded a prize.

5. For a list of winners (available after 3/31/92), send a separate stamped, self-addressed envelope to: Silhouette Fashion A Whole New You Sweepstakes, P.O. Box 4665, Blair, NE 68009.

PREMIUM OFFER TERMS

To receive your gift, complete the Offer Certificate according to directions. Be certain to enclose the required number of "Fashion A Whole New You" proofs of product purchase (which are found on the last page of every specially marked "Fashion A Whole New You" Silhouette or Harlequin romance novel). Requests must be received no later than December 31, 1991. Limit: four (4) gifts per name, family, group, organization or address. Items depicted are for illustrative purposes only and may not be exactly as shown. Please allow 6 to 8 weeks for receipt of order. Offer good while quantities of gifts last. In the event an ordered gift is no longer available, you will receive a free, previously unpublished Silhouette or Harlequin book for every proof of purchase you have submitted with your request, plus a refund of the postage and handling charge you have included. Offer good in the U.S. and Canada only.

SLFW-SWPR

SILHOUETTE® OFFICIAL SWEEPSTAKES ENTRY FORM

4-FWSRS-2

Complete and return this Entry Form immediately – the more entries you submit, the better your chances of winning!

- Entries must be received by **December 31, 1991.**
- A Random draw will take place on **January 30, 1992.**
- No purchase necessary.

Yes, I want to win a FASHION A WHOLE NEW YOU Sensuous and Adventurous prize from Silhouette:

Name _____ Telephone _____ Age _____

Address _____

City _____ State _____ Zip _____

Return Entries to: Silhouette **FASHION A WHOLE NEW YOU,**
P.O. Box 9056, Buffalo, NY 14269-9056   © 1991 Harlequin Enterprises Limited

PREMIUM OFFER

To receive your free gift, send us the required number of proofs-of-purchase from any specially marked FASHION A WHOLE NEW YOU Silhouette or Harlequin Book with the Offer Certificate properly completed, plus a check or money order (do not send cash) to cover postage and handling payable to Silhouette FASHION A WHOLE NEW YOU Offer. We will send you the specified gift.

OFFER CERTIFICATE

Item	A. SENSUAL DESIGNER VANITY BOX COLLECTION (set of 4) (Suggested Retail Price $60.00)	B. ADVENTUROUS TRAVEL COSMETIC CASE SET (set of 3) (Suggested Retail Price $25.00)
# of proofs-of-purchase	18	12
Postage and Handling	$3.50	$2.95
Check one	☐	☐

Name _____

Address _____

City _____ State _____ Zip _____

Mail this certificate, designated number of proofs-of-purchase and check or money order for postage and handling to: Silhouette **FASHION A WHOLE NEW YOU Gift Offer,** P.O. Box 9057, Buffalo, NY 14269-9057. Requests must be received by December 31, 1991.

ONE PROOF-OF-PURCHASE

4-FWSRP-2

To collect your fabulous free gift you must include the necessary number of proofs-of-purchase with a properly completed Offer Certificate.

© 1991 Harlequin Enterprises Limited

See previous page for details.